ICEBOX

A. B. Richards

Based on a True Story

PUBLISHED BY:
Black Mare Books
Houston, Texas
www.blackmarebooks.com

ISBN: 978-1-941502-53-2
Icebox
Copyright © 2017 by Artemis Greenleaf

Acknowledgements

I would like to give a big shout-out to the Houston Public Library – what an amazing resource for newspaper clippings and other historic resources.

As always, thank you to my wonderful family. This endeavor would not be possible without your love and support. I also appreciate the invaluable editorial and structural help of my critique groups and beta readers. You know who you are, and I couldn't do this without you. Finally, a big thank you to the law enforcement officers I've had the opportunity and privilege to interact with.

The past is prologue.

-William Shakespeare

Other Books

by A.B. Richards

Rescue: A Litter of Quetzels

1

Houston Homicide Detective Quetzel Cazares squatted at the base of the shattered live oak tree. A yellowed, dirt-encrusted skull stared up at her. Square chin. Prominent brow ridges. Probably male. She'd seen plenty of skeletal remains during her career, and she was right about gender more often than not. The Harris County Medical Examiner's office had begun setting up a grid for excavation of the bones.

"Wonder how old this tree was?" Cazares asked.

"No idea," replied Cooper Morgenstern, an investigator from the ME's office. "How long has the Dome been here?"

Cazares' knees cracked as she stood up. *Getting old is hell.* She gave the dingy grey hulk of the Astrodome a long sideways look. Blue and red strobes from the police vehicles reflected off the puddles in the parking lot, and NRG Stadium employees who had come out to see what the yellow crime scene tape was all about stood in small clumps just beyond the barrier. A black plastic trash bag and a neat stack of assorted aluminum cans were tucked into the shrubbery behind one of the other trees. *We must be standing in the parlor of a person who had no place else to go at night. Sad, with all the money in this town.*

Cazares got her smartphone out and did a quick search. "Dome opened in 1965. Maybe somebody planted our decedent here at the same time as the trees. That lightning strike was a one-in-a-million shot."

Cooper nodded, and stared at his instruments.

"You've never been to a scene this old, have you, Coop?" Cazares asked.

He shook his head. "I'm not sure my mother was even born when this site was fresh."

Cazares chuckled. "I don't imagine there'll be much evidence to collect before the Skeletal Recovery Team gets the bones out of the ground and back to the lab. I've got fresher corpses that need my attention, though."

Back at her office, Cazares took a sip of her coffee and opened the case folder for the skeletal remains found at the Astrodome. A soon-to-be-eaten sandwich hid amongst the piles of folders stacked on her desk.

The forensic anthropologist estimated the bones belonged to an adult male, forty to fifty years old. His clothes had largely rotted away and most of the items in his pockets had decomposed beyond recognition. A handful of coins with dates from the 1950s and 60s; three bills too ruined to identify without serious technology; and a fragile, folded piece of paper with faded ink were the only contents of a long-gone pocket. Inside his wallet, there was enough of a driver's license left to determine that his last name was "__gers," but the number, date and picture had been obliterated – they weren't laminated back then. Curiously, there was a metal frame with the blackened remains of a Polaroid photo. The roots of the tree had grown through the decedent's ribcage, indicating that the body had been buried underneath the tree when it was planted – the spring of 1965.

Cazares started by trying to match the remains with any missing persons from that year, but came up empty. Then she started on open case files from 1960 to 1965.

"Well, would you look at that?" she said out loud.

Dmitri Ilyn prairie-dogged up over the next cube. "What you got, Quetz?"

"Come see for yourself."

He rounded the corner to her cluttered desk and peered over her shoulder at the forensics report, then to the cold case file beside it.

"The Icebox Murders? Seriously?"

"What's that?" Tenner Morrison had just come back from the break room and held a tepid cup of stale coffee. He'd been Quetzel's partner for the past six years, and they had one of the highest clearance rates in the department.

"Quetzel may have just found the prime suspect in the Icebox Murders."

She had to read the murder book to refresh her memory – the Ice Box Murders were a local legend, but no one ever tried working the case because everyone involved was dead. DNA evidence wasn't a thing in 1965, and even if the blood samples from the crime scene were not degraded and unusable, there were no known existing samples of the suspect's DNA to compare them with. Unless there was an unspoiled, notarized confession in his pocket, there was virtually no chance of proving anything.

The facts of the case, few as they may be, were:

• June 23, 1965, the nephew of an elderly couple, Fred and Edwina "Ebbie" Rogers, requested a welfare check on them.

• Two Houston Police officers entered through an unlocked back door and found the house unoccupied.

• There were no obvious signs of foul play.

• Officers opened the refrigerator and noted a large quantity of fresh, unwrapped meat inside. Neither officer considered that it might be human remains, until the heads of the elderly couple were discovered in the vegetable crisper.

• Charles Rogers, the couple's forty-three year-old son, was missing.

• Drops of blood led to his attic bedroom, and a bloody keyhole saw, as well as a Colt Huntsman pistol, were found inside.

• He had never been located, and was declared dead in 1975 so his estate could be probated. *About ten years too late, apparently.*

• Charles was extremely reclusive, and most neighbors were unaware that he lived at the residence.

• A witness reported that Charles had picked up some dry cleaning on Saturday, June 19.

• Detectives concluded that the murders occurred on Father's Day, Sunday, June 20, because the victims were known to be alive on the 19th, and a Sunday newspaper was found inside the residence with blood spatter. Subsequent editions were left in the yard where the paperboy had thrown them.

• Charles had been a naval intelligence officer during World War II, and worked for Shell Oil as a seismologist, before quitting his job in 1957 for no apparent reason.

Still, finding these remains, if they did belong to Charles, did nothing to clear up the mystery. It would be between difficult and impossible to confirm that the remains belonged to Charles. For all she knew, they belonged to a completely unrelated "__gers." Even if the bones were Charles', it didn't prove that he didn't commit the murders. But he certainly didn't plant himself under a tree on the grounds of the former Eighth Wonder of the World. As no one ever saw him coming or going from his house, it would have even feasible that Charles could have been dead for years before his parents were killed, were it not for the dry cleaning pick up the day before the murders. But then again, Quetzel had never had a dry cleaner ask to see her ID when she'd picked up clothes.

One theory was that Fred and Edwina were abusive towards Charles, and he'd finally gotten fed up and killed them, then fled the country. But Charles was a grown, competent man. Why would he walk away from a stable, high-paying job to not only go live with his abusers, but be completely dependent on them? That didn't make sense. But what if he had been debilitated in some way? He'd apparently been perfectly healthy when he slammed the door on his employer.

She shook her head and got back to the report from the ME's office. She almost choked on her next sip of coffee, then picked up the phone.

"Are you telling me," she said when she finally got Miranda Taylor, the forensic pathologist, on the phone, "that the DB had cancer?"

"Looks like it. Lesions on the bones are consistent with metastatic carcinomas. I can't say whether it killed him, but he did have it. A number of the lesions are quite large, deforming the bone, which suggests to me that it was in an advanced stage. Did you also notice in the report that there was no evidence of decomp in the soil samples we took?"

"You think the body had decomposed before it was brought to the site?"

"Possibly. Of course, the body has been there a long time, so perhaps the soil markers have dissipated. Sterols don't persist forever. The tree would have taken up those nutrients over the years, too. Oh, and there's one other thing. The decedent had once broken his left arm – the ulna, just past the wrist. It was well healed, so it probably happened when he was a child."

When Cazares hung up the phone, she closed her laptop. It had already been a long day, and this case was making less sense with every new scrap of information she got. Besides, she had to go home and feed her kitten, Gato.

She had never considered herself a cat person, but she found a kitten – tiny, black, and starving - at a crime scene, and she couldn't just leave him there. He'd turned out to be a good pet. He kept her company by sitting in her lap and purring, or supervising the work that she invariably brought home with her. Once, he'd even given her the inspiration to solve a case. Besides, having him forced her to go home from the office at night – before that, she had been known to crash on the sofa in the division lobby on occasion.

The drive from downtown Houston to Cazares' house wasn't bad, usually less than half an hour, if there were no accidents on the freeway. She tried to think of what she needed to do on her day off, but the Rogers case kept popping up instead. Finally, she gave up, and started turning it over in her head, trying to see an angle that no one else has seen before. If the pile of bones in the ME's office belonged to Charles Rogers, the Ice Box Murders suspect, who killed him, and why? Had he been mentally ill, hiding in his room and slipping notes under the door for his parents? Or was he incapacitated by cancer? Was it even Charles in Charles' room? If he didn't butcher his parents, who did? So far, the evidence was circumstantial that the remains belonged to Charles. If this was a completely unrelated case, she had even less information to go on.

Unfortunately, the only people who could answer those questions had been dead for half a century.

Gato met her at the door, meowing, when she came in. Quetzel secured her sidearm and put it in the end table drawer next to her recliner before she scooped the little black kitten up. He purred loudly as she carried him into the kitchen. He rubbed his cheeks against her chin and kneaded her arm with his claws. She gave his chin a little scratch before she set him down so she could open a can of food. She always left dry food out for him, given that her schedule could get weird at a moment's notice. It had always disappeared by the time she got home. She just assumed he was making up for lost groceries, given how skinny he was when she'd rescued him.

"Keep your fur on. I'm opening it as fast as I can," she told him as he rubbed against her ankles. She poured the contents into a bowl, and Gato made his usual strange growly *nom noms* as he gulped down the food.

A thud came from the living room. Gato paused and looked toward the door for a moment before resuming his meal. Quetzel went to investigate. The Fred and Edwina Rogers murder book lay on the floor. A picture of a young man in a US Navy uniform had separated itself from the rest of the papers and gazed cheerfully up at her. *I was sure it was in the middle of the coffee table. How did it get on the floor?*

She took her Glock out of the drawer and took off the safety. The front door was locked. Quetzel searched room to room, but she was the only person in the house. She returned to the living room, but instead of replacing the gun in its drawer, she left it on the table next to her. The idea of someone being in her house unsettled her. She was not a fearful person, but every day presented her with plenty of evidence that evil ran rampant in this world. She held her breath for a moment, listening, then picked up the file and snapshot.

Charles Frederick Rogers. The missing son. Maybe not missing any more. She studied the photo. Average looking, not quite handsome, but not unattractive, either.

He did have a very square jaw, just like the skull she'd held in her hands earlier. Quetzel checked the file for his medical records. Nothing. This work up was made long before the digital age.

One thing caught her notice: The Rogers family had been involved in a single car accident in Gonzales, Texas, in August of 1929. Charles' older sister, Betty had been thrown from the vehicle. She was transported to the local hospital, but pronounced dead. Could Charles have broken his arm then? Maybe. Hopefully Dr. Singh's office could find out.

Gato did not like the man with the fedora hat. He'd shown up when Quetzel brought in that thick binder. There was something not quite right about him, but he didn't seem to be dangerous. Although with humans it wasn't always obvious. It was clear to Gato, though, that the man had been dead a long time, and he was desperate to tell Quetzel all about it. She, of course, couldn't see the man, even though he stood right beside her recliner as she flipped through the book.

The kitten licked his paw, then rubbed his ear. He would keep watch. Quetzel protected him, so he would protect her. As the Centurions used to say, it was *quid pro quo*.

2

The zoo had been a sticky, sweltering mess. Charles never liked going there, and especially not having to ride in the stifling car for hours from Houston to San Antonio to do it. Betty always felt sorry for the animals, especially the monkeys, trapped in concrete and steel cages. It made her sad, and if she was sad, Charles was sad.

Betty was three years older, and to him, his ten year-old sister was practically an adult. She taught him to pretend to be asleep when their father's drunken rages brought him storming down the hall, spoiling for a fight. She had taught him how to breathe slowly, silently through his nose when hiding was a better option. Their parents doted on Betty, and gave her favors and sweets that were denied to Charles. Betty always shared her bounty with him. She loved him, whether or not Fred and Ebbie did. His sister did not mind his strange ways. Even if he didn't like being touched, much less hugged, she understood him. She smuggled books from the library for him to read. He especially loved the science ones.

He wished he had one now. And a light to read by. The Texas August was too fierce to drive in for long stretches when the sun beat down on the plain, so the family travelled at night. The loud Model A engine throbbed and clattered as it puttered down the rutted highway. The windows were rolled down to keep the family from suffocating, and the occasional June bug jittered in, buzzing and bumping against the windscreens and the upholstery. Betty squealed each time one crashed into her and scratched her with its prickly feet.

"Shut up, or I'll give you something to scream about!" their father growled from the front seat.

Charles clenched his fists, but he could do nothing. Someday, when he was bigger and stronger, he would be able to stop Fred's violence. Someday. Even their cousin, Raymond, cringed against the seat when Fred shouted. He was the same age as Betty, but got along better with Charles.

Grandma Rogers had fallen sick, and the family had made the drive to San Antonio in what was probably a final visit. Ebbie took the three children out to the zoo while Fred struggled to make peace with his mother.

Charles didn't like Grandma Rogers. She smelled strange and her voice was raspy and hard to understand. She also did not like children.

The last gas station between San Antonio and Houston was in Gonzales, so Fred pulled over to top off the tank. Snacks eaten, legs stretched, and car refueled, they set out for home. On a smooth, straight road, the Model A could go as fast as sixty miles per hour. But the

Old San Antonio road was neither. Sharp turns, unbanked curves, and potholes kept their progress much, much slower.

Charles tried to sleep, hoping they'd be home by morning. He closed his eyes and attempted to get comfortable, but it was no use. And he knew better than to complain —nothing could be done but suffer through it.

He tried making up a story inside his head.

Suddenly, Ebbie screamed. Charles and Raymond were slammed against the back of the front seat with Betty on top of them. He couldn't tell what was happening. Gravel crunched and popped against the chassis of the car. With a heart-stopping thump, the car left the road and rolled over twice. As everyone tumbled around, Charles couldn't be certain whether he was right side up or upside down. The car came to a stop on its side.

People moaned and cried – Charles couldn't tell who was doing what. All he knew was that he had to find his sister and make sure she was alright.

"Betty," he called softly. He got no reply. He tried a little louder. Still nothing. He moved Raymond's legs off of him and sat up. That's when the pain hit him. A searing ache in his left arm, just above the wrist. He sucked in a deep breath and tried not to cry. He failed. He needed Betty even more desperately now. It was dark inside the car, and he could see almost nothing.

"Get out of the car," Fred rasped as he started climbing out of the open driver's window.

Charles scampered out his own window as best he could with one arm. His legs were shaking and he feared he'd fall out at any moment.

His mother helped to push an unconscious Raymond out of the window, but Charles wasn't paying attention. Something white back near the ditch shone dully in the moonlight. He couldn't tell what it was, but icy dread snatched at his stomach. Cradling his injured left arm in his right, he stumbled over the uneven ground to the white thing. As he got closer, it came into focus.

"Noooo!" he wailed. Sobs rattled his thin body as he knelt beside his sister. She looked like she was asleep. "Wake up, Betty." She didn't move. He shook her. Her hair and face were sticky with blood.

Footsteps crunched in the crisp grass behind him. Ebbie screamed and threw herself on the ground. Fred tried to pick her up, but she fought him off.

Charles did not know how long he sat there in the dark next to his sister, listening to his mother crying and his father shouting. His father had brought along a friend to help with the driving, but Charles didn't remember his name. He felt he should learn it and never, ever forget it, because he had been at the wheel when the car left the road.

After a while, flashing red lights punctured the gloom. Police first, then an ambulance. Betty was strapped in, small against the stretcher, and loaded into the vehicle. Ebbie went with them, leaving Charles to fend for himself, as always.

Betty's white casket was so small. Charles thought that maybe she wasn't really in it after all, and the whole thing was nothing but a big prank. Betty would jump out of the choir loft, smiling, and everyone would scold her for being so cruel, then they would all laugh. The service dragged on. She did not come out. Four men carried the little coffin out to the hearse, which headed to the cemetery, followed by mourners. She must be outside, behind a tree, he reasoned. His stomach felt sick. The joke had gone too far, and he was ready for it to be over. His arm, wrapped in cotton and ACE bandages, throbbed in the August heat.

Pallbearers lowered the casket into the gaping hole, and handfuls of earth were tossed onto it. The mourners left. Betty never appeared.

Sometimes, Charles would dream about Betty. She'd put her arms around him, and in his dreams, it wasn't uncomfortable. She'd tell him stories and remind him of where to hide when Papa's scary friends came over. He'd wake with tears in his eyes because he needed her so much in this physical world.

Neither Fred nor Ebbie ever directly told Charles that they wished he'd been killed instead of Betty. But he knew it was true. Knew it because he had the same wish.

3

Alright, Detective Swann. What does this site tell you?" Quetzel asked.

Tenner's wife was having surgery, so he'd taken the next two weeks off. Freshly minted Detective Amanda Swann would be riding with Quetzel while he was out. Since she came from the Gang Unit, Swann had seen a number of death scenes.

Swann ran a hand through her closely-cropped red hair and looked around the room. The decedent, Mrs. Adriana Garcia, had already been taken to the morgue. All that remained was a pool of blood and a scattering of numbered yellow evidence markers.

"This will be cast-off." She pointed to droplet trails along one wall and the ceiling and paused to count. "Looks like twelve distinct tracks, so she was stabbed at least twelve times."

Basic stuff. "So far, so good."

"These drops over here by marker three, they're round, so that's gravity. The killer probably stood over his victim after the attack, and blood dripped onto the floor."

"Whose blood?"

"I guess it could be either, if the knife slipped and he cut himself."

The two women moved over to another evidence tag.

"I'm not too sure on this one. A few plastic and glass fragments. And to be honest, with the state of this house, I'd question how recent this was," said Swann.

Cazares chuckled. "Good point. But the debris is from her cell phone. Looked like it had been smashed up against the wall. They've already taken what's left of it to the IT guys to see if there's anything on there we can use."

"And how did you know that?"

"Well, after a while, you get to know all the folks in the Crime Scene Unit. Remember that officer I talked to when we first got here? He told me."

"I thought you were just asking about his new baby, and I felt a little awkward, since I didn't know him. That's why I walked away. I just didn't think…"

"And you've worked how many death scenes so far?" Quetzel asked with a smile.

"This will be my second. As a Homicide investigator. Not sure how many I've seen in Gangs. A lot."

Quetzel nodded. "You'll be able to match up all the documented evidence with the photos once you get the file, but it's good to get an idea of what's going on before that. Once in a while, it's the littlest thing that cracks the case. The CSU folks are pretty good at pointing stuff out, if you talk to them."

Quetzel's phone rang.

"Cazares."

"Got a DB for you. South Loop. It's been there a few days."

"Hold on."

Quetzel fished a notebook with a pen stuck in the spiral binding out of her bag. "Alright, go."

"7000 block of Cayuga Street. People walking a dog found a body behind the warehouse."

"We're on the way."

She disconnected. "Let's get finished up here. We've got another one."

"Busy day."

"Yeah. Mrs. Garcia's husband is off getting stitches for cuts on his hand. We'll interview him later. After that, we'll come back and talk to the neighbors, see if we can confirm his story. Responding officers already took their statements."

"Looks like a domestic dispute gone wrong."

"Could be. Most of the time crime scenes are exactly what they look like. But not always. Don't assume anything – if you do, you may end up trying to make the facts fit your theory instead of the other way around. And that always comes back to bite you in the ass."

The death scene lay just a little south and east of the well-heeled Medical Center, and Quetzel drove down 288, arguing with her GPS navigator. Once she got to Cayuga Road, it was easy to drive to the flashing lights. A thin line of trees separated the warehouse from a large, empty lot. There was a lot of space between buildings here.

Yellow crime scene tape decorated a section of shrubs and trees. Two women with a dog stood under a half-dead live oak tree, talking with patrol officers.

"They must have found the body. Let's have a look at our decedent before we talk to them. Something to keep in mind: it's not uncommon for suicides to find a secluded outdoor location to pull the trigger. Don't want their families to have to clean up the mess."

Cazares and Swann made their way around back. The first thing Quetzel noticed was the smell. She pulled a bottle of mentholatum rub from her bag and dabbed a little in each nostril before offering it to Swann, who shook her head.

"You sure about that?" Cazares asked.

"I don't need any, thanks."

"Suit yourself. Oh, and Swann? Watch your step. Sometimes people have a strong reaction to a crime scene, especially with…a more decomposed body. You don't want to get puke on your shoes."

Swann nodded.

The corpse had been baking under the Houston sun for a while. Maggots churned underneath the bloated, green and purplish-brown skin. Patches of long, dark curly hair were scattered around the remains. A ragged hole gaped at the top of the skull, which lay on top of the chest. The decedent's arms and legs has been disarticulated and were lying haphazardly around the torso. The decomposition was advanced enough that it wasn't possible to tell the corpse's race or gender, as it was difficult to tell if there were any parts that should have been there, but weren't.

Swann stopped walking. "Probably not a suicide, then."

"Probably not." Cazares snapped on a pair of nitrile gloves and squatted near the pile of remains. "Have you ever seen anything like this?"

Swann shook her head. "No. The ones I've seen have been pretty fresh."

"You look a little pale. Why don't you go sit down, maybe put your head between your knees?"

"N-n-no. I'm alright." Swann swallowed hard.

Cazares shrugged and turned back to the dismembered corpse. "Look at the size of these maggots." She scooped out a few on her gloved finger. "They're pretty big – body has probably been here five to seven days, but the bug people can say for sure. If the decedent was on drugs, it can affect their size."

Cazares redeposited the larvae and stood up. "You can see marks on the exposed bone – I would guess the killer used a large, serrated knife or maybe a saw to disarticulate. And I doubt this hole, "she pointed to the skull, "was caused by scavengers. I'm interested to see what the ME comes up with." She peeled off her gloves. "Swann?"

Quetzel turned to see the rookie detective lying in the grass. She sighed and made her way over to her prone colleague. "Swann! Amanda?" Cazares shook Swann's shoulder. "Wake up!"

Swann groaned and sat up.

"Come on. Up you go." Cazares reached out her hand.

The younger woman accepted the gesture and let Cazares pull her up. "I'm sorry. That was so embarrassing."

"Don't worry about it. That smell can be overpowering. The first time I saw an advanced decomp, I lost my lunch."

"No. It wasn't the smell. I had a car accident years ago and fractured my skull. I completely lost my sense of smell. The body just looks so…gruesome. Blood doesn't bother me so much – but maggots? Eech!" Swann shuddered.

"Well, not being able to smell anything could be an asset for working Homicide."

Swann couldn't help giving up half a smile.

They went back to the front of the warehouse where the women and the dog stood under the tree with a patrol officer. A small clump of bystanders stood outside the yellow tape. From their dress, Quetzel figured at least a few of them were working girls – not rare creatures in this area. The Crime Scene Unit had arrived, and she waved at the tech who was unloading equipment.

Quetzel turned back to the witnesses, the two dog walkers. "Good afternoon. I'm Sergeant Cazares, and this is Detective Swann. We need to ask you ladies a few questions."

"We already talked to these cops. Can't you get it from them?" the older of the two women grouched.

"Well, ma'am. I certainly will. But I may have different questions for you." Quetzel smiled and took out her notebook.

"I just want to go home," the younger woman wailed.

"Yes, ma'am. I understand. I think we can speed up the process if you go sit in the AC in that patrol car – front seat, of course – with Detective Swann, and I'll talk to your friend with the dog out here."

The younger woman turned to her companion, who pursed her lips, but nodded anyway.

Over the years, Quetzel had found it easier to separate witnesses at a scene if she made it sound like she was doing them a favor. She smiled at the dog walker.

"What's your name, ma'am?"

"Virgie."

"Is that your first or last?"

The woman huffed. "What do you think? It's short for Virginia." Her head wobbled from side to side slightly. "Beech. Like the tree. Virginia Beech."

"Thank you, Ms. Beech." Quetzel wrote in her notebook. The dog, a medium-sized black and white pup who may or may not have had a border collie parent, wagged its tail and came forward to sniff at Quetzel's hands. She ignored the pup, and it lowered its head to sniff at her pant leg. The dog yelped and jumped backward cowering behind its owner.

"What did you do to my dog?" Virgie growled.

Quetzel frowned and picked a black cat hair from her khakis. This was the second time a dog had reacted that way to her in the last week. She made a mental note to research cancer sniffing dogs. Just to make sure.

"I'm not sure what happened there. I didn't touch him - maybe he stepped on something?"

The lady glowered. "What do you wanna know? I'm already missing my shows." She fixed her glare on her companion a dozen yards away in the patrol car. "I told Lurleen we shouldn'ta waited for the po-lice."

"Yes, ma'am. Sorry for the inconvenience. Could you tell me exactly how you discovered the body?"

"Lurleen and I was walking Skippy, like we usually do, you know. And he run off and wouldn't come back. We went around the back of the building to look for him. That's when we saw it."

"And do you usually walk the dog in this area?"

"Nah," Virgie answered. "We usually go the other way, but they got the sidewalk blocked off 'cuz they got road work going on thata way."

"Okay. Have you heard about anybody from this neighborhood going missing in the last week or so? Maybe someone with long dark hair?"

Virgie rolled her eyes. "People go missing in this neighborhood all the time. Mostly because they cain't pay their rent, so they skip out before their stuff gets locked up. Sometimes 'cuz they're in jail. Don't know if you noticed, but this ain't River Oaks."

Cazares glanced at the derelict buildings. *I've noticed. Believe me I have.* Then she looked at the patrol officers. "You have their contact info?"

One officer held up a metal clipboard.

"Thanks for your cooperation, Ms. Beech. If you happen to remember anything, please call me." Quetzel handed her a card. "You're free to go. If we have any further questions, we'll be in touch."

"I didn't know you were working cold case files," Swann said, running her fingers over Fred and Ebbie Rogers' murder book.

"Normally, I don't, but we seem to have unearthed the missing person of interest."

"How about that?" Swann picked up the binder and flipped through it. "Navy guy, huh?"

Cazares heard her suck in a quick breath, and looked up.

"Now that's just weird."

"What?"

"You're working on a cold case file with people being chopped up and stacked in the fridge, and we just came from a death scene with a dismembered body. Spooky, don't you think?"

4

The advantage to having the top corner rack was that he didn't have to share with anyone. Most of the beds were always in use – day shift slept on them at night, night shift during the day. He could not have tolerated strangers in his private space like that. The idea of it made him shudder. At 5'7", Charles Rogers found the quarters less cramped than most of the other sailors. It also made the cockpit of the *SOC Seagull* he flew that much roomier. And he liked that well enough.

The *Seagull* was practically a relic – it had come into production in 1935, and it was a biplane, for Pete's sake! The new jet planes, now those were the ticket. Although, if he were pressed, he would admit that he liked the open-air cockpit. The wind on his face exhilarated him. He'd been flying scout and observation missions for Naval Intelligence since he'd been assigned to the USS Richmond. The only thing he didn't like about it was his observer. Tom Finnegan spent a lot more time flapping his gums than he did observing, that was for sure. That loudmouth bragged about doing things he'd never actually done, and got sore when anyone called him on it.

One of the greatest pleasures of his current life, Charles found, was cleaning this palooka out at card games. Finnegan was a lousy blackjack player, and even worse at poker. Charles just saw taking his money as due compensation for having to endure his company during scouting missions.

There was little to see on the escort route from the Galapagos Islands to Chile, aside from orcas and whales – he wasn't sure what kind they were, though. Physics was his bailiwick, not biology. Besides, there were no enemy warships in Patagonia.

The USS Richmond had put in at Valparaiso, Chile, for supplies and refueling that morning. In the afternoon, the sailors, desperate for R&R, surged ashore. The brightly painted buildings and mishmash of European colonial architecture went unnoticed as the shipmen sought out women and alcohol, not necessarily in that order.

Charles wasn't interested in either. Or at least not alcohol. He'd seen how the eel juice could bring out the eels in his father's head, and he wanted no part of that. As for women, he was interested, but he wasn't good at talking to them, and was so rarely lucky that he didn't even try. Sure, he could pay for a pro skirt, but he didn't have any rubbers, and he was also disgusted by the thought of sloppy seconds (or thirds). Even the remotest possibility of dipping his wick in the same pond as the likes of Tom Finnegan made his skin crawl. That didn't mean he didn't mind window shopping. He just wasn't planning on buying.

The Hotel Alemán had been fancy, last century. Now, the thick carpets were faded and threadbare. The plaster was cracked and water stains decorated the ceilings like abstract frescos. Once-grand hotel or not, the bar smelled like any other bar. Ghosts of decades worth of cigarettes lingered in the drapes, and the greasy fetor of last week's fried food haunted the wallpaper. Charles sat in the back corner, sipping yerba maté out of a gourd, watching.

Ladies with low-cut blouses chatted up men, then sooner or later, the price agreed, the happy couple made their way upstairs. Most of the girlies weren't hard to look at, but with a ship full of seamen in town, any able Grable could rake in the cabbage. Charles nursed his tea, and his bitterness.

He had just about decided to head back to the Richmond when she walked into the cantina.

Her blue-black hair tumbled nearly to her waist, highlighted by a green, orange, and red-striped skirt. A belt made of seashells slung low on her hips reined in a loose cotton tunic. The light at her back shone through the translucent white top, making Charles wonder if an angel had decided to swoop in and rescue them all from the debauchery going on around him. Once the door closed behind her, she looked like an ordinary peasant girl. A doll, for sure, though, and he wondered why none of these ginks gave her a second look.

He watched as she spoke with the barman. She pulled something out of the pocket of her tiny white apron and handed it over, but Charles was too far away to see what it was. He didn't think she was a working girl. A few more words with the barkeep, and she turned and left. Charles had already made up his mind to head back to his ship anyway, so he stood up and set his maté on the table. He went to the can first, then stepped out into the street. He could have hailed a hack, sure, but decided to save the cab fare and walk. It wasn't that far, and his pins could use a stretch.

His brain buzzed with ideas as he strolled towards the harbor, and he paid little attention to the shops and shoppers in his path. A high-pitched scream pierced the veil of his thoughts. Some heads turned in its direction, but only Charles ran towards the sound. He heard it again, and was sure it must be coming from a nearby alley.

He jogged to it, only to find the chick from the bar. Two sailors had her backed up against a wall.

"Hey!" Charles shouted. "Knock it off, you big lugs. Scram!"

The two would-be assailants turned tail and ran. *Cowards.*

"You okay, Miss?"

She ducked her head. "Yes. Yes, I am unharmed."

Charles had a flash of inspiration. "You know, those mugs could be anywhere. Would you like me to escort you home? I'm Charles, by the way. Charles Rogers."

"Thank you, Charles Rogers. I would like that." She had a Spanish accent, but her English was perfect.

"Well then," he said, offering her his arm. "Let's go."

Walking close to her, he breathed in her aroma. It was earthy, but not in the way of leaf mold and dirt. Instead she smelled of petrichor, as when rain finally quenches parched earth. He inhaled as deeply as he could without being obvious about it, savoring the smell. *Is it possible to get drunk off the smell of a woman?*

She led him up the hill, away from the harbor, but he hardly noticed. Closely clustered buildings thinned out, and finally, they arrived at a rustic shack at the periphery of the city. The young woman opened the door and gestured for him to come inside.

Charles balked. He wasn't one to trust strangers, and although there was clearly no one inside the one-room house, someone could be lurking around the back waiting for him to be in a vulnerable position so they could sweep in and rob him.

"I don't even know your name," he said coyly.

"Is that important?" she asked.

Charles sighed inwardly. *Just another working girl, after all.* "Yes, ma'am. To me it is." He turned to go.

"Orco Mamman," she said. "That is what I am called."

"Yes, ma'am. I have to get back to my ship."

"Betty sends her regards."

He whirled to face her. "Betty?"

"Your sister. She died when you were seven. She is well, but she worries for you. She only wishes you to be happy."

"I don't understand. How do you know about Betty?"

Orco smiled. "I know many things." She approached him slowly, deliberately.

She reached over and caressed his face with her soft hand, and a seismic tremor of pleasure shook him to his core.

Charles looked deeply into Orco's eyes for the first time. They were a dark amber, flecked with gold. His head spun. Suddenly, Charles had the sensation of falling, and tried to catch himself against the doorframe. His hand scrabbled at empty space.

Now, it seemed both of them were floating, swirling, tumbling inside a massive fire that pulsed and throbbed around them. Charles felt no heat, only the early tinglings of ecstasy. His breath quickened. Orco moved around him, and he could not tell where he ended and she began. He became liquid fire, bright and blinding.

It wasn't clear to him if the words were spoken aloud, in his head, or even who said them. but what he heard was, "Gold is forged in the heart of a star."

Then he shattered into a million tiny suns.

When Charles woke up, he lay in his rack, with no idea how he got there or how much time had passed. He was startled by the roughness of the wool blanket against his skin. *Had it always been so scratchy?*

A voice called his name, in a whisper that echoed in his skull. It tugged at his solar plexus, beckoning him to come. He slipped out of the bunk and followed the pull. On the bottom bed, four berths over, a sailor snored, his left hand on top of the covers. A gold wedding band shone in the dark, as if it were a glittering strip of starlight.

5

Quetzel floated up from sleep, gradually becoming aware of the hissing of the kitten in her lap. He growled as menacingly as a four-pound kitten can. She opened her eyes and realized she was in her recliner and hadn't even managed to turn off the floor lamp. Fred and Ebbie's murder book lay open on the coffee table. Gato stared at the back window, ears pinned, back arched, and tail fluffed to maximum. He growled again.

Quetzel listened, but heard nothing. Everything beyond the pale curtains was still. The detective set the hissy kit down and got up, turning on the outside floodlights and pulling back the curtains.

A June bug buzzed against the glass, and a translucent gecko scurried away from the glare. Quetzel closed the drapes and shut off the lights. "Well, whatever it was, you must have scared it off, eh kit-cat?" She scooped him up, but he refused to be soothed, so she let him go.

There wasn't much point in getting up and going to bed – a glance at the clock told her it was three AM. 3:07 to be exact, but who was counting?

"Don't touch that remote! There's more!" the infomercial pitchman barked from the TV.

Quetzel picked up the remote, settled back into the recliner, and turned off the lamp. Gato quickly reclaimed his warm spot in her lap. Growls turned to purrs as he kneaded her abdomen with his claws. She scratched his chin, then raised the remote to shut off the television. Something made her pause, though.

"Not only can you own your very own shares in a proven portfolio of gold mines, but, if you act now, you can qualify for our exclusive energy portfolio! It's like a license to print money!"

The salesman babbled excitedly as images of bobbing pumpjacks, spewing dollar bills, rolled across the screen. A badly Photoshopped picture of a man who may or may not have been Venezuelan strongman Hugo Chavez lounged on a stack of gold bars.

Quetzel snapped the light back on. She scooped Gato up in one hand and retrieved the murder book from the coffee table. Charles Rogers had worked as a seismologist, locating oil deposits. He also consulted on gold and mineral mining locations on the side. He'd spent time in Central America. Could he have acquired a tropical illness while he was there that had debilitated him enough to force him to move back in with his parents? She sent a quick email to Cooper Morgenstern in the ME's office to ask if there was a way to tell if that could be the case, given that they only had skeletal remains.

🐈

It didn't take long for Quetzel to fall back to sleep after typing on her cell phone. Gato knew the man in the backyard was watching, waiting for his opportunity. One of the first things that Quetzel had bought when she'd brought Gato home was a lock for the doggie door. It hadn't taken Gato more than five minutes to figure out how to defeat it. He let himself out into the backyard and made his way straight toward the man squatting behind the air conditioning condenser unit.

"Mraaow."

The man slapped at Gato. "Get out of here, you stupid cat."

Gato wrapped both paws around the offending hand, sinking his claws into the man's skin. He bit the man's thumb hard enough to draw blood, and raked his back claws against the man's wrist.

"Son of a-" He grabbed the little cat by the scruff of the neck and tried to pull him off. "Let go!" he snarled through gritted teeth.

But Gato did not let go, and the man tried to smash him into the wall. The space was too narrow to get a good swing, so he stepped out from behind his cover, Gato scratching and biting the entire time.

"I'll fix you, ya little shit." He raised his arm to bash the kitten against the bricks, but his shoulder was nearly wrenched out of joint. The cat suddenly weighed more than the man could lift.

Gato let go of the man's arm. It was in his way. He purred, a low, thrumming sound from deep in his chest. He stood eye-to-eye with the man now, a hulking beast out of darkest nightmares. The man's jaws worked frantically, but only a broken whimper came out. That wouldn't do – he might find his voice and scream, waking Quetzel. Eyes glowing green, the feline snatched the burglar's throat in his wicked teeth and clamped down tightly until the man went limp.

Dropping his prey, Gato grinned as only a cat can, and licked his lips in anticipation. This body was soft, so it would be tender and well-marbled, much tastier than any stringy legionnaire had ever been.

Quetzel was about to get into her car for the morning commute when her phone rang. It was her daughter, a senior at the University of Texas at Austin. Bianca had a job and her own apartment, which her father paid for, and she hadn't come home for the summer since freshman year. She usually only called on Thursday afternoons.

"Bianca? Is everything all right?"

"Sure, mom. I wanted to catch you before you got tied up with work. Did I?"

"Just leaving. What's going on?" Quetzel slipped into the car and put the phone into its cradle for hands-free mode.

"I have big news."

"Did Stanford accept you into the grad school program?"

"I haven't heard back yet. It's something else – something even better. Justin popped the question last night."

Um, yippee? She's been dating that shady Justin Forrester for nearly two years now. Is he finally going to give up his grey-market hustles get a real job? In spite of his parents having money, a dollar never sticks to him, slipping through his fingers as quickly as it comes — spent on whatever shiny new trend caught his eye: tattoos, ear plugs, nose piercings, skinny jeans, and flannel. I think he's moved in with Bianca, anyway — easier to leech off of her that way. But if I say a word about it, it's only going reinforce her attachment to him. At least, that's how it had worked throughout those awful high school years.

"That is big news."

"You don't sound happy about it."

"It surprised me. I wasn't expecting that at all. Have you set a date?"

"Yes. August the twenty first."

"That's less than a month away."

"I know. I wanted to have the wedding before I started to show."

"Hey, Quetz. We sent off DNA on your dismembered DB. There's something kind of odd, though," Cooper Morgenstern said.

Quetzel had her phone on speaker. "What's that?" She was still reeling from her daughter's announcement, and struggled to keep the annoyance out of her voice.

"When we looked at the disarticulated joints, the cuts appeared to have been make with a small saw. But Dr. Singh noticed an unusual residue, so we put it under the micro. Any guess as to what it was?"

"No."

Morgenstern paused. "Chitin."

"Chitin. Okay. And that tells us what, exactly?"

"Chitin is what bugs and crustaceans use to build their shells. It's embedded in the bones, so it didn't get there from normal entomological activity."

Cooper couldn't see the brow that arched above Quetzel's left eye. But she was fairly sure he could hear it in her voice. "Seriously? Are you trying to tell me that a giant bug cut him up in the park?"

"No. I'm saying that chitin is embedded in his bones."

"Fantastic."

"And another thing. There is no ocular tissue in the skull."

Quetzel's lip curled. "His eyes were missing?"

"Yep."

She sighed inwardly. "If the killer spent that much time with the victim, I won't be surprised if more show up."

Quetzel procrastinated as long as she could. She never, ever called Jorge unless it had something to do with the kids. And why would she? There were a multitude of reasons he was her ex. She went into an empty interrogation room to call him.

"Quetzel? What's up, Baby? I sent a check to Bianca last week." He doted on his kids, Bianca and Indigo, even if he had fallen out of love with Quetzel. But he never quite let go of his ownership of her, a claim she refused to recognize.

"When did you talk to her last?"

"Is she okay?"

"That remains to be seen." She fumed inwardly at Bianca, who had not only ambushed her this morning with her news, but set her up to have to call Bianca's father. She'd never given up on throwing them together at every opportunity. Whether it was out of spite or hopes they'd find their way back to each other, Quetzel couldn't tell. Even after Jorge remarried – to a woman only two years older than Bianca – her daughter seemed to delight in creating awkward situations between them.

"She called early this morning to tell me she's getting married."

"*¿Que?* To who?"

"Guess."

"Not that Forrester pendejo."

"Who else?"

Jorge swore in Spanish.

Quetzel waited until he stopped cursing. "It gets better. She says she's pregnant."

There was a long, drawn out sigh from Jorge's end of the conversation. "This is your fault."

"How is this my fault? She's twenty-two years old. We could barely contain her when she was fifteen."

"And that's because you worked all the time, instead of being home like a good mama."

Quetzel was glad that he was miles away, at his car dealership. If he were in her office, she would have struggled not to slap him across the room for that.

"And I suppose your running around with any tramp that would spread for you was a great example for your kids. Call your daughter." Quetzel clicked the phone icon to disconnect, wishing she had an old-fashioned receiver to slam down in his ear.

People are afraid of the murderous stranger. But most homicide victims are killed by people they know. Quetzel understood exactly why this was so.

Her cell rang. The caller ID said "I.C. Deadppl."

Quetzel was just relieved it wasn't Jorge. "Hey, Coop."

"You okay, Quetz? You sound a little down."

"I'm fine. What have you got for me?"

"Name of your decedent, the dismembered one. Thomas Philip Edwards, a white male."

Given the long hair at the crime scene, Quetzel had suspected the DB was female. But lots of men had long hair. She wrote down the rest of the information about Tom Edwards so she could retrieve his records.

Coffee called, burnt and stale though it might be. Quetzel stood. Her cell phone rang.

"Mom! I have to talk to you. It's really, really important."

6

Charles tossed in his rack, unable to fall back asleep. He lay there, stifling in the warm, stale air. His pulse throbbed in his ears. *What just happened? Am I losing my mind?* Charles could still feel the pull on his solar plexus, like a string tugging at his vitals. Only now, there were more strings pulling in more directions. *Make it stop.* He reached out with trembling fingers and gingerly probed his stomach, expecting to find raw open wounds, entrails creeping to the surface. But his fingers only touched taut, unbroken skin. He pulled in a shuddering breath, mouth open to minimize the noise. He could not tell how long he stared at the bulkhead inches from his face before exhaustion took him and he lapsed into an uneasy slumber.

"Charles? Charlie-boy?"

"Where are you?" he called. Charles turned around, fog clouding his vision. Vague outlines of trees loomed in the twilight. But underneath one bright green oak sat a girl of ten years, glowing bright against the gloom. She lounged on a red and white checked blanket with a wicker picnic basket in front of her.

"Over here, silly," she beckoned.

"Betty? It's been so long." He sat down next to her.

"I know. I'm sorry. But, little brother, you've gone and got yourself in a real doozy of a spot this time, and I mean sure enough."

Charles shook his head. "I don't understand what's happening to me."

"You've been given a gift, Charlie-boy. But you have to use it real careful. If you do that though…well, you'll see. Don't be scared, just be smart, got it?" She opened the basket and pulled out a perfect red velvet cupcake. Charles smiled. He could always count on his sister to remember his favorites. He took it from her, inhaling the sugary waft of icing. His lips parted, tongue anticipating the first taste of creamy frosting.

Instead, cold water splashed over his face. He jerked upright, banging his head on the steel bulkhead, then swore loudly.

"Rise and shine, flyboy. Briefing in ten."

"Yes, sir!"

Charles scrambled into his uniform, swished a little water around his mouth to loosen the plaque, and ran up the ladder to the ready room with a scant minute to spare. Nothing would happen until they'd cleared the harbor. Even then, their mission was the same as always, and there were no enemy ships on this side of the Pacific. At least not yet. He focused on the wedding ring that shimmered and flashed on the commander's hand whenever he moved. The strings pulled at Charles, demanding he get closer. He struggled to resist as the boss man droned on and on about the mission that was the same as the last one, that was the same as the one before that.

After the briefing, Charles' stomach rumbled. If he hurried, he still time for mess, so he headed to the galley for breakfast. He came around the corner and stopped in his tracks.

Standing there, haggling with the chief steward over a few crates, stood the bartender from the Hotel Alemán.

Charles flattened himself against the bulkhead. When the barman stepped out of the supply room, the pilot stepped in front of him.

'Hey! What do you want? Your cook already robbed me – I have never got such a low price on my vegetables." His eyes narrowed.

Charles reached into his pocket and brought out a wallet, then fumbled it open and pulled out a fin. The barkeep squinted at the $5 bill, suspicious.

"I need some info. What's the dope on that bird from the bar yesterday? I know she gave you something – I saw it. Told me her name was Orco."

The bartender pushed Charles' money away. "I can tell you nothing about her."

"Can't or won't?"

The barman shrugged and tried to push past.

"Please," Charles begged. "I need to know."

Heaving an exasperated sigh, he said, "Walk with me."

The two men headed for the gangway. "She is not one to be trifled with," the barman said.

A little late for that. "What if some trifling has already taken place?"

Two sailors came around the corner, and Charles and his companion fell silent until they had disappeared around the next bend.

"If she deems you worthy, she might provide you with a gift."

"Like what she gave you in the bar?"

"She brought me herbs and a crystal for my sister, who is ill. And it was not a gift – I paid her from them."

Charles frowned. "Then what kind of gift do you mean?"

"Have you any idea who she is?"

"Just a broad who lives in a shack on the edge of town."

The barman chuckled. "You are very wrong, my friend."

Charles huffed. He was tired of the barkeep's evasion. "She did something to me. I want it to stop."

"You cannot return a gift from Orco Mamman. It is yours for life. Unless…" he chewed his lip.

"Unless what?" Charles didn't even try to hide that he was losing patience with the bartender.

"You have no idea what she is. You think she is an ordinary woman. That could not be further from the truth. There are those who might consider her a goddess – she is the protector of all things that come from the earth, but do not grow. Diamonds, silver, that sort of thing."

Like gold? Charles absent-mindedly rubbed his solar plexus.

The barkeep continued, "She can gift you with the ability to locate anything from her domain. But you must never get greedy and take too much. Then the blessing becomes a curse that will eat you alive."

"A curse, huh?" Charles' studies in physics and geology made him particularly disinclined to attribute supernatural agency to everyday occurrences. "I think that's a load of applesauce."

They reached the gangway. The bartender turned slightly toward Charles with half a pained smile. "Applesauce or no, I would not cross Orco Mamman."

As he walked away, Charles called after him, "Yeah, I'm sure she's just the darb." He could see the barman's head shaking, but he did not turn or reply.

A sailor wearing a thin gold wedding band walked by, and Charles felt the strings pulling him towards it. He frowned and went below.

7

What's wrong, Bianca? Are you alright?"

"Of course I am. I made an appointment for you. Write this in your calendar and make *sure* you don't miss it. Do you know how hard it is to get an appointment at Valentino's?"

I don't even know what Valentino's is. "And what is this appointment for?"

Bianca sighed dramatically. "Your dress fitting. Really, Mother."

"Can you text it to me?"

"Fine. Bye."

Moments later, the text chime sounded, and Quetzel added the event to her calendar. *What is this, an episode of Bridezillas?*

Now that Bianca's crisis was, at least momentarily, averted, Quetzel got back to her work. The decedent du jour, Tom Edwards, was not the sort of man anyone would want their daughter to date, not according to his rap sheet, but he hadn't deserved to be butchered. Pandering. Assault. Petty theft. Definitely not a nice guy, but none of those were capital crimes. She'd originally thought he might have been at exactly the wrong place at the wrong time and encountered a serial killer. But now she wondered if maybe he'd crossed the wrong person and they'd made an example of him. Wouldn't be the first time.

She absently wound a few strands of hair around her finger as she studied the crime scene photos. *How did you get here, Tom? What made somebody make you look like this?*

Quetzel rubbed her eyes.

"Shhhhh!"

The detective whipped her head around just in time to see a dark object drop from the AC vent in the ceiling. If she hadn't rolled her chair back, it would have fallen on her. A dark orange scorpion stood on her desk and menaced her with its pincers and uncurled its tail. She exhaled.

"Where did you come from?" Quetzel picked up her empty coffee cup, flipped it and trapped the arachnid underneath.

Dmitri peered over the top of his cube. "What was that?"

"Scorpion fell out of the vent. If you hadn't made a noise, it would have landed in my lap." She slipped one of the sample wedding invitations that Bianca had given her under the cup and turned it right-side up. The incensed arthropod scuffled inside the mug.

"Wasn't me. I didn't make any noise." Dmitri came around the side of the cubicle to peer into Quetzel's cup. "What are you going to do with it?"

She replaced the card. "Let it go outside."

The ghost of a smile floated across his lips as he shook his head. "Only you, Quetzel. Only you."

There was a church a couple of blocks away. Their flowerbeds were the only greenery in the vicinity that Quetzel knew of, so she made her way there. A few late-working paper mites straggled out of their offices toward the train stop. Phones in hands, they never even noticed she as there. She dumped the scorpion at the base of the wrought iron fence. It brandished its pincers one last time before it scurried into the azaleas.

She hadn't gone half a block when her phone rang. *Shouldn't evening shift be taking calls now?* "Cazares."

"Flintbridge. We've got another DB, same MO as the one you're working. Can you come out to the scene?"

"Of course, Lieutenant. What's the address?"

Perhaps she'd been hasty in putting her serial killer idea on the back burner. The body was in the same state as Tom Edwards'. This one had been found by a jogger, and was more disordered. Something had disturbed the pile of parts, probably a dog, given the paw prints in the sand around it, and the head had rolled into the nearby ditch.

Lieutenant Flintbridge met her at the crime scene perimeter. "We sent his prints off, but he's got enough gang tatts that we've tentatively ID'd him based on those. Vincente Aguilar is the only one in Gang's database with a blue teddy bear over his heart."

Quetzel shook her head. "I would think so. You found his head, couldn't you compare his photos?"

"No."

"No eyes, severe blunt force trauma?"

Flintbridge nodded.

So did Quetzel. "Sounds like the others."

"Others? I thought this was the second one."

"The one we found last week, and there's another with the same MO that's a cold case. Three cold cases, possibly, but I can't tell if the other two are related. Not much to go on. The victims were never identified."

"How cold?"

"1965 – the Icebox Murders – have the same MO, well, mostly. The other two are 1962 and 1964 – not much to go on there."

"That's more than fifty years ago. You think you're looking for a seventy-something year-old serial killer?"

"At this point, I don't really know what I'm looking for."

"I hope you find it soon, because if the paper picks up on this, there's going to be a panic."

.8

Charles thought that getting back into the sky would be just the ticket to get him out of the blue funk that embraced him like a bitter lover. Spring in Alberta was not warm, certainly not by Houston standards, anyway, and the chill reminded him too much of his tour of the Aleutian Islands in the winter of 1943. He tried to forget about the battle of the Komandorski Islands that following spring. It had only lasted four hours, and the USS Richmond hadn't suffered any direct hits, but he reckoned it was the closest he'd come to death since that terrible car crash that took his sweet sister away from him.

Over time, Charles had learned to turn down the volume on the call of gems and precious metals – gold wedding rings, gold fillings surrounded him. Instead of a constant tugging at his solar plexus, it was more of an unpleasant tickle, like ants crawling just beneath his skin.

One thing he hadn't learned to control, however, was the pull of hydrocarbons. Oil in the ground caused a sharp yank at his middle that made him want to vomit.

Gas. more subtle, made his head swim. Refined petroleum products – like kerosene and motor oil, were more like white noise in the background, the difference between a wolf and a chihuahua.

He'd worked out how to tell exactly what kind of treasure was near by the sensations it gave him. While that made it hard to sleep, it also made his life vastly more comfortable. His father was a spendthrift on things for himself, but stingy with money for the household. Ebbie was miles off being a saint, but she was his mother, and she'd done the best she could for him, even if her best wasn't very good. He didn't want to see the old woman on the street. His new-found abilities allowed him a side business of gold and gem prospecting that gave him the greenbacks to pay for his parent's house. The oil company he worked for had a sweet profit-sharing deal for its exploration team, with royalties on discovered fields. Charles never missed a big find.

That's why he sat in a Cessna now, flying over Canadian hydrocarbon prospects. He couldn't tell them the real technique he used, so he told his bosses that there were certain geological markers he looked for. How many times had his manager told him he should write a white paper about his method? "Sure, sure. I'll do it later." But later never came. And the company was so busy producing oil and gas that they let it slide. He wasn't feeling anything though. Not here. He wondered if he should choose a site, anyway. He'd just found five fields in a row – a statistical improbability. He had to have a dry hole once in a while, just to keep things from being too many standard deviations off normal.

He scratched at his belly. Poison ivy? He'd been in the woods a few days ago. But how could he have gotten poison ivy there, underneath his coat and shirt? Perhaps it was a bug bite.

The purr of the engine and the eagle's eye view of the Canadian Rockies failed to soothe him. He tapped his middle finger on his notebook. Maybe it was the date he had tonight that made him so unsettled. Sweet and tiny, Abigail worked at the restaurant near his hotel in Medicine Hat. He stopped for breakfast at the Maple Kitchen every day on his way into work, and he'd gotten quite friendly with her as she waited his table. If her section was full, he'd wait until a table cleared. One day, he'd jokingly asked if she'd like to go to the picture show with him to critique Marilyn Monroe in *The Seven Year Itch*. She'd said, "Sure thing, Chaz." Charles found himself growing much fonder of her much faster than he'd ever intended. He knew that when winter came, he be headed back down south. Should he ask her to join him?

Callahan's wasn't the most expensive restaurant in Medicine Hat, but it wasn't far off. Dinner and drinks for two could set him back almost ten dollars.

The steaks were ordered, and the waiter had just brought their green salads and poured their cabernet. Charles raised his glass to Abigail. She blushed and copied his movement. The hash house she worked in didn't serve booze of any sort, just breakfast and lunch. She didn't have much experience with fine dining, and he was more than happy to teach her everything he knew.

Abigail plunked her glass down, sloshing a few drops of red wine onto the crisp white tablecloth. Her hand flew to her mouth. "Oh, gosh!"

"Don't worry about it. They get wine stains out all the time."

She nodded, not entirely convinced. But her dull mood left as quickly as it came. "Chaz! Guess what?"

She was the only person, except for Betty, who'd ever called him anything other than Charles. He liked it, coming from her. "What's that?"

"My dad got his receiver today!"

"His what?"

"Receiver. He just got his ham radio license, so he ordered the radio kit. He's putting it together tonight and tomorrow so he can try it out over the weekend. I'm going to help him with his QSL cards."

"Sounds Greek to me, baby." Charles smiled as he shook his head.

Abigail took a bite of salad.

"The cards are like, when you talk to another operator on the radio, you and the other person write down each other's handles and stuff on a postcard, then mail them to each other. After a while, you have a big box of cards from everywhere. Neat-o, huh?"

Abigail's enthusiasm was contagious, and they talked of very little besides ham radio during dinner. As interesting as Charles found Abigail's enthusiasm for riding the amateur airwaves, he was enthusiastic for something else.

Charles eased the cork out of the bottle of chardonnay. *Rock Around the Clock* blared from the radio as he poured.

Abigail jitterbugged over to the small table to pick up her glass. "We should go out dancing once in a while, you know?" She wrinkled her forehead. "You got grease or something on your shirt."

"It's nothing, baby. Oil from the cowling – we were flying earlier." Charles raised his glass to her. "You'd be the star on the dancefloor, doll. I got two left feet."

"Oh come on! It's a snap once you get the hang of it. I'll show you." She took a sip from her wine glass and set it back on the table. "C'mon." She grinned and opened her arms to him.

He took a gulp of his drink, set his glass next to hers, and moved into her embrace.

"Not like that!" She giggled.

The song changed. Abigail stood next to Charles, trying to get him to do the Twist with her. He struggled - his knees didn't seem to work that way.

The music changed again. "This, I know." He slipped his arm around her waist, pulling her close as Les Baxter crooned *Unchained Melody*. They swayed to the music, shuffling their feet more or less in time to the rhythm. Abigail rested her head against Charles' shoulder, and he caressed the small of her back. She sighed with contentment, so he kissed her. He liked the way she melted into his arms, and his lips moved from hers to her neck. He'd never been a fan of being touched, but this, he could do. A lot. Abigail untucked his shirt and ran her hand across his abdomen, her wrist grazing the growing bulge in his slacks. She inhaled sharply and pulled away.

"Charles? What is that?"

He laughed softly and murmured, "You know what that is."

"Don't be a goof! This." Abigail had found the rash.

Embarrassment scorched Charles' face. "I think it's just a bug bite. Seismic team was out in the woods a couple of days ago." He tried to pull her close again, but she resisted.

"A bug bite? Then why is it wet?"

"Wet?"

She pulled up his shirt and gasped. Charles looked down and swallowed hard. Not only had the rash spread, but now it was oozing a black, oily substance. "It...it wasn't like that earlier," he stammered.

"Let me call Dr. Peterson to come look at that."

Charles tugged his shirt back down. "It's late. I hate to call him out now."

Abigail scowled. "Promise me you'll go to his office tomorrow, then." She found the notepad he kept by the phone and wrote down a number. "I should probably go."

Even though he was disappointed, he really couldn't blame her. Who would want to play mattress polo with someone leaking black pus? "Let me at least walk you home."

"Sure thing." She washed her hands in the kitchen sink before pulling on her jacket.

She held his hand, but didn't walk as close to him as usual. When they got to her door, she kissed him – a peck on the lips. They were in public after all. "You will go see the doctor tomorrow, right?"

Charles thought her attempt at an authoritarian face was adorable, and he tried not to smile. "Cross my heart and hope to die."

"Don't say that! This could be serious. I mean it, Chaz. Call the doctor."

"Yes, ma'am. I'll take the day off tomorrow. Promise."

"You'd better." She caressed his cheek. "I have to go. Mrs. Thomas across the street is watching. She'll call my mother and give her a report."

"I'll call you tomorrow and let you know what the doc says."

"I've never seen anything like that." Dr. Peterson frowned at Charles' midsection. The gauze pad he'd taped over the weeping rash was already saturated with thick, black fluid. "If I didn't know better, I'd say it was...oil." He shook a test tube containing a sample of the liquid. He'd also taken tissue samples for a biopsy. "I'll send this off to the lab in Calgary. In the meantime, I'm going to give you a salve and prescribe penicillin, eh?"

That was a week ago, and Charles had taken every pill, exactly as the doctor directed. He slathered on smelly sulfur ointment twice daily. The rash had spread. He'd taken to folding a pillow case into quarters and taping it to his abdomen to absorb the drainage. Nobody knew about it, except for Abigail. He called her nearly every day, but didn't dare ask her out again, not until he found out what caused the rash. If it was contagious, he'd never forgive himself if she caught it off him. He even stopped eating meals out; instead, he cooked for himself on a sad hot plate in his room.

Charles almost didn't stop by the office that afternoon. He'd been out with the seismic crew all day, working on a land survey, and he was exhausted. Charles spied a note on his desk from the department secretary: "Call Dr. Peterson."

The lab results must be in.

·9

Quetzel stood near the door, cold coffee in hand. It was just as well that she was tired of sitting – the conference room was SRO, given that it was all-hands-on-deck, now that a third body had turned up. His prints had identified him as Marvin Peckinpagh, only notable to police due to being caught in a vice squad prostitution sting two years ago.

"I don't have to tell you how much the mayor wants this whack-job off the streets." Chief Anna Haskie never came to their murder squad sessions – why would she? But then again, she'd never had a brazen serial killer loose on her watch, either.

Right now, they had found precious little trace evidence – no hair, no fibers, no prints. The only thing left by the killer was chitin fragments in the separated bone ends of the disarticulated joints.

If they could find the locations where the killings took place, that would be something. There had to be clues there. Right now, though, there were three butchered corpses, and the city was on the threshold of panic.

"The Criminal Analysts are working an experimental software that's supposed to triangulate the killer's home, based on the body dump sites, so make sure that you get every detail to them ASAP. We've also requested support from the Feds' Behavioral Analysis Unit – the agent's on the way. We will get this guy. Let's just make it sooner rather than later."

The Chief and her detail swept out of the room.

Detectives and investigators slowly got up and milled around. Doing nothing was not an option, but their paltry leads had been hashed and re-hashed into oblivion. Quetzel went to the large whiteboard and re-read the bullet points.

1.   All victims male
2.   All victims had eyes gouged out
3.   All victims had been drained of blood, dismembered, and left in a public place
4.   All had traces of chitin in the bone abrasions
5.   No apparent connection between victims.

Not entirely true – a petty criminal, a gang-banger, and a john.

Quetzel spotted her partner, Tenner Morrison, talking on his cell in the corner of the room, so she made her way over to him. His skin matched the faded grey paint on the walls, and the bags under his eyes qualified as luggage.

"Okay…I know." He sighed, and the corners of his mouth turned down slightly. "Make sure the doctor's office calls it in – I'll pick it up later...Okay, bye." He ended the call.

"Tenner? You okay? How's Gladys?"

"Not so good. She's having some complications from the surgery. Her sister came down to stay with her, since my medical leave got revoked."

"I didn't know they could do that."

Morrison shrugged. "Apparently they can."

"Well, you tell her I said she's not allowed to be sick."

Morrison almost smiled.

"Hey."

Swann had approached so quietly that Quetzel hadn't seen her until the last second. She nodded to the new arrival. "Let's go over the death-scene photos again. I've got a Mother-of-the-Bride dress fitting at lunch time."

Quetzel frowned at her reflection in the full-length mirror. "Surely, Bianca, there's another color you like besides pastel yellow." The shade made her look washed out and sallow, and the shapeless skirt that hung below the empire waist screamed 'maternity dress!'

The sales lady nodded. "Yes. I think the periwinkle would be more complimentary for your mother's skin tone. And she looks nice for her age. Show her off with a fitted bodice, yes?"

Bianca pouted. "I like the yellow. It matches the flowers."

"I'm sure Tawni-leigh will appreciate your efforts to make me look hag-like."

Bianca snorted, then quickly suppressed her laughter and rolled her eyes. "Mo-THER. Fine. Try the periwinkle."

Still a petulant teen, even though she's twenty-two.

The sales lady handed her the dress, and Quetzel disappeared into the fitting room. When she returned, the sales lady clapped her hands together. "Bravo! Yes, that is the dress for you." She opened the door and called, "Janice! Bring the pins!"

A dark-haired lady with a shy smile entered, pincushion strapped to her wrist and tailor's chalk in her hand. There wasn't a lot to do — the dress fit reasonably well off the rack.

"Tut, tut!" Janice muttered as she inserted a pin into the bodice and Quetzel flinched.

She looked for a clock. There wasn't one. They still had to fit Bianca's dress, and neither she nor the sales lady seemed interested in moving the whole process along.

After all the pins were pinned and the hems were chalked, veils, slips, petticoats, and shapewear were trotted out and selected, Quetzel made a point of looking at her watch.

"Is there anything else at all that I can help you with?" The sales lady asked, with a broad smile.

What else could there possibly be? Quetzel shook her head. Bianca hugged her hand-beaded gown.

"The receptionist will take care of the deposit for you." The sales lady gestured to the front of the store.

The fashionably-dressed young lady at the reception desk printed an itemized receipt and handed it to Quetzel.

"Yes, ma'am. And which card would you like to use for the $4,250?"

"I thought we were just putting down a deposit."

"That is the deposit."

Quetzel looked at the full-page list of wedding apparel. *How much of this could we get rid of?* This seemed like an awful lot of money to spend on a one-hour ceremony to start a marriage that was never going to last. Quetzel shifted her bag off her shoulder so she could open it. *That $8,500 would do a whole lot more good at the women's shelter. Am I really thinking this about my own daughter's wedding?*

"I have Daddy's credit card." Bianca flounced up to the receptionist with a Platinum American Express in her hand.

Quetzel smiled on top of her clenched jaw. Why was she not surprised that Bianca had let her squirm for a minute, knowing the whole time she had Jorge's card? Her daughter hadn't rolled very far from the paternal tree. About one thing, Jorge was right. This was Quetzel's fault. She should never have been taken in by him – all the red flags had been there. But she'd spent most of her twenties in the Air Force and her biological clock was ticking loudly. And he'd been so charming. At first. By the time she was pregnant with their second baby, Indigo, she was too deeply ensnared in Jorge's traps to just walk away. It took time to get out.

Was Bianca marrying Justin so she could produce grandchildren to please her very traditional father? He never put Indigo under that kind of pressure. In fact, he bragged that his son was finishing up his Bachelor's degree at prestigious Rice University in only three years, and had already been offered a full scholarship to Harvard College of Medicine. Bianca was just as smart as her brother, but not nearly as driven. At least not overtly. And that's what worried Quetzel. What, if anything, was she harnessing that brain power for in secret?

Quetzel hugged her daughter. "I really have to get back to work. Love you."

10

Honduras was sticky. And hot. Charles wished that their exploration took them south, into the mountains, to escape the liquid air and the brutal sun of the northern coast, but it was not to be. Sweat soaked his clothes and ran down his face. He grunted as he swatted at a mosquito that whined around his ears. There was oil around here. The pull on his midsection told him so. Unfortunately, it was all offshore. There was a new barge that could drill in twenty feet of water, and the industry scuttlebutt had it that a Mobile Offshore Drilling Unit that could work in forty feet of water was being developed. But he didn't think even that would help – the connection felt cold, far away. Charles couldn't be sure, but he thought the reservoir was probably closer to Mexico than Honduras. His employers wouldn't be happy about that, but what could he do about it?

Pulling his canteen out of his pack for another sip of lukewarm water, he wondered if Abigail shivered in the January Canadian snows, missing him as fiercely as he missed her. He liked to think that if he'd asked her to come with him, she would have said 'yes.' But he hadn't asked her. He could never ask her.

Charles remembered how he had sat fidgeting in the uncomfortable guest chair as the somber doctor gave him the bad news. There were abnormal cells in the biopsy they'd taken of his weeping rash. Dr. Peterson had told him that perhaps they'd caught it early enough that surgery would remove the lesions and the cancer cells wouldn't metastasize and spread throughout his body, sinister vagrants staking out toxic campsites. The good doctor had no explanation for the greasy black fluid that wept like filthy tears from his sores, and looked and smelled suspiciously of oil. In the end, Charles was sent to a surgeon who removed a four-inch square patch of flesh from his abdomen. The wound was still raw, and even the gauze padding didn't keep out all the stinging sweat. He kept his diagnosis a secret, even though he probably should have manned a desk while the surgical wound healed. Charles was rotting from the inside out, and he couldn't bring himself to tell anyone, especially sweet Abigail. She would have taken care of him – he was sure of it – but he couldn't put that on her.

He'd seen people die of cancer. It was an ugly death, its victims wasting away a little more each day, finally too weak to do anything more than lie in their own filth. No. He would not put Abigail through that. Better for her to despise him as a cad than watch him die like that. Charles stumbled and twisted to catch himself, wincing as the stitches pulled against his scabs. The flash of pain swept away his reverie and snapped him back into the unhappy present.

"We should probably make camp here for the night," the guide said. It was some time before dark, but there were tents to pitch and mosquito netting to hang, for all the good it would do.

Dinner had been better than Charles could have reasonably expected, and he'd gotten drowsy working on his reports. If he could just rest his eyes for a minute... He leaned his chin on the palm of his hand and let his lids droop.

It felt like an insect, or other small vermin, crawled through Charles' hair. He slapped at it, then gingerly probed his scalp with his fingers, looking for a tiny carcass. He found something, but it wasn't tiny.

In his hand lay a thick clump of his own hair, matted with black pus and patches of scalp.

Charles recoiled and dropped it, losing it in the folds of his shirt. His hands flew to the crown of his head. More hair came away in his fingers.

The metal shaving mirror. *Where was it?* He scrambled for his kit and snatched it out, not caring that the other contents scattered across the ground. His hand shook so hard that he nearly dropped the polished metal plate. Lumpy nodules the color of old bruises erupted from his skull, oozing black fluid. A strangled sob escaped his throat.

"You were warned."

Charles whipped his head around to see the shape of a woman standing at the back of his tent in the dark. "Who are you? What are you doing here?"

Her eyebrow quirked upwards. "Don't you remember me?" Her voice was soft, her words sliding into his ears and slipping around his brain like silk.

That voice. Of course, he remembered her. How could he forget? She stepped into the dim circle of lamplight.

Long, dark hair.

Eyes like the stars on a moonless night.

He had been looking for her for a long time. His mouth hardened. "You did this to me, Orco. Why? For the love of God, why?"

"Be very careful when you invoke the gods. You might not like the results. I rewarded your good deed with a gift. Do not blame me for your misuse of it."

"Please. Please take this away. I'll do anything you ask." His voice broke. "Anything."

"It's too late. There is nothing I can do." The half-smile that moved across her lips fell far short of her eyes. "However, it may be that if you can control your greed, you may have a measure of control over your symptoms."

Charles hurled the mirror into the pile of spilled belongings. "Greed? What greed? What have I done —"

"Why are you here?"

"What?"

"Why. Are. You. Here? In this place, right now?" Orco's eyes blazed with fury.

Unable to withstand her glare, Charles looked away, his gaze resting on the reports he'd been filling out.

Perhaps she was right.

"I'll quit. As soon as I get back to the States, I'll walk into the boss's office and say, 'I quit!' I won't show 'em any more oil. No treasure. Nothing."

"It's a start."

11

Three red map pins stuck out of the map where the bodies had been found. All of them had lain inside a rough rectangle that was bordered on the west and south by the bend in the 610 Loop, the east by Highway 288, and north by U.S. 59. Quetzel placed the fourth pin in the same sector and drew a mental outline, starting with the first body found. Did the killer live somewhere within that shape? She needed another cup of coffee. The daily newspaper sprawled across the table, and front-page headline didn't help.

SOUTH LOOP BUTCHER BAFFLES COPS

Early this morning, a fourth dismembered body was found in southwest Houston in the 2700 block of El Camino Street. A jogger discovered the remains just before dawn. Multiple law enforcement agencies have been working the case, but police have

```
few leads. Chief Anna Haskie urges
citizens to remain calm.
```

The article continued, detailing the three other murders. The ME's office hadn't even identified the decedent yet. Quetzel sighed. A media frenzy wasn't going to make her job any easier.

The task force was now made up of what seemed like half of Homicide, a sprinkling of Gang and Vice officers, three Texas Rangers, and a handful of Feds. Anybody that could be corralled to work on it had been. But this was like many other murder investigations. Nobody saw anything. Nobody knew anything. Nobody was usually their star witness.

Quetzel went over the crime scene photos again and again, lining them all up on a whiteboard in columns, one for each decedent. But no amount of squinting or photo reshuffling revealed any more clues. The signature was unmistakable, though.

Skull crushed.

Eyes gouged.

Limbs disarticulated from the body.

Blood and internal organs missing.

Left in a public place.

Chitin was the first thing she asked Cooper to confirm when they picked up this latest body. Just to verify it wasn't a copycat. The first DB had been a pimp, the second two were customers. Queztel would be surprised if John Doe #4 didn't fall into one of those categories – being a homicide victim is often a lifestyle choice. Hang out with bad people, and bad things tend to happen.

Swann tapped the table between Quetzel and Morrison. "Hey, I'm going to run out for coffee. Want me to bring you anything?"

"That'd be great." Quetzel grabbed her bag and reached for her wallet. "Double espresso large mocha, soy milk, cinnamon, no whip. And one of those sandwiches – whatever looks the freshest." She laid a twenty on the table.

Morrison also reached for his wallet. "Same for me. Except real milk. None of that soy shit."

Swann picked up the money. "All right. Back in a few."

Quetzel put her bag away. "How's Gladys doing?"

Morrison closed his eyes and softly shook his head. "Not good. She's back in the hospital. Can't keep her blood count up. Doc thinks there's an internal bleed."

Quetzel squeezed his shoulder. "Then why are you here? Go."

Morrison hesitated, but Quetzel gestured towards the door. "I'll talk to Flintbridge. Go on, get out of here. You might even catch Swann in the elevator."

Morrison nodded, then headed toward the door, and Quetzel turned back to the whiteboard and absently tapped her pen on her jaw. "Where are your clothes?"

"Trophies."

Her head snapped toward the speaker. She hadn't realized she'd asked her question out loud. "Excuse me?"

A young man stood off to her right. The credentials around his neck were FBI issue, but she wasn't close enough to read the name. Some of the tech guys were local, and this was probably one of them – Behavioral Analysis hadn't arrived yet. "Serial killers often take a trophy from their victims."

Oh, please. Quote more textbook passages for me. "Or maybe they are where the murder actually took place, instead of at the dumpsite."

"Possibly."

"So has that computer program of yours come up with the killer's name and address yet?"

The agent eyed her, probably trying to gauge whether she was truly hostile or just stressed. "We've had some successes with the software. It's got built-in artificial intelligence that's pretty impressive, especially when combined with a detailed profile."

Quetzel nodded, staring at the photos and wondering what she had missed.

Her phone rang.

"Cazares."

"Yeah. This is Riley over at Southwest. We picked up a homeless guy this afternoon who claims he knows the John Doe who was cut up in the park this morning."

12

Charles had bought himself two fedora hats, one grey, one brown, before he left Honduras. He always wore one or the other, and never took it off, not in public, anyway. He ignored the glares and mutterings. "Son, you don't wear a hat where it don't rain." But they'd like it even less if they could see the oozing, misshapen mess that his head had become. They should be grateful for small favors.

It took him a week to write up what he claimed to be his methods for finding hydrocarbons. He went into detail about geological markers and salt dome extrusions. There was an article he'd once read about that. He didn't mention Orco Mamman's cursed gift. Now that he was about to hand it off to his boss, he felt an odd mixture of anxiety and relief. He had no idea what he was going to do once he quit his job.

"I need to see Mr. Spencer," Charles said to the secretary wearing rhinestone cat-eye glasses.

"He's on a phone call." She nodded toward one of the angular leather chairs that bookended a massive potted fern.

Charles sat. The secretary made a carbon copy sandwich – blank white paper, carbon paper, yellow paper – and rolled it into the typewriter. The machine clattered as her fingers danced over the keys. His mind wandered – what would his boss say when he handed in his notice? Would he be angry? Indifferent? They hadn't always gotten on, but Charles' ability to find oil made him a valuable asset.

"Drat!"

The secretary's exclamation startled Charles, and his head swung in her direction. She got out her eraser pencil with the brush on one end and rolled the paper out of the typewriter a few lines.

The door opened, and Mr. Spencer came out of his office. "Myrtle, can you – oh. Hello, Rogers. Is there something you need?"

Nope, just sitting here for my health. "Yes, sir. I have that whitepaper you wanted. And I need to speak with you about another matter, too."

Spencer sighed and looked at his Rolex. "Come in then. Myrtle, could you get me that Mexico file?"

Charles followed his boss into the extravagant office. It mirrored its occupant – all style, little substance. Thick white drapes hung from floor to ceiling, muting the natural light and diffusing it against the dark oak paneling. A five-shelf bookcase, crammed with books Charles doubted that Spencer had ever read, loomed above the minimalist steel desk.

"I have an appointment in twelve minutes. Speak."

"Um…I…I have the document you wanted, about my oil-finding methodology." Charles handed the file folder over, and noticed a damp mark from his hands.

"So you said." Spencer dropped the folder onto his desk without looking inside. "What was the other thing?" He looked pointedly at the gold-plated clock on his wall.

That made it easier, since he clearly wasn't wanted here. "Sir, in that folder, you'll also find my resignation. Effective immediately."

"You're quitting? Any specific reason why? You do remember that your employment contract has a non-competition clause."

"I'm not going to work for another company. I'm just leaving. That's all."

"I will very much miss your strike rate. At least you left us your procedure. I'll call security to escort you out. They'll meet you at your office." He picked up the phone receiver and started dialing.

"I'll just see myself out, then."

Charles felt a weight lift off him as he walked out the door. "Afternoon, Myrtle." He tipped his hat to her, ever so slightly, as he passed.

He'd already taken home the few personal items that he kept on his desk. A small framed Polaroid of Abigail. His old, chipped coffee cup. A walrus-tusk scrimshaw from his days in the navy. The only thing he had to hand over to the two beefy security guards was his ID badge. Lifting that lanyard felt like releasing an albatross from around his neck.

There was a coffee shop around the corner from his apartment. He stopped in for a cup of joe and a little time to think. Charles doodled and scratched notes on a napkin as he stared out the window, watching the traffic go by. His rent had just been paid, but perhaps he should give his landlord notice. Sure, he had royalty checks coming in, enough to cover the rent and buy groceries, but he may need that money for doctors soon. *Ha. Who was he kidding?* How much time did he have left? A month? A year? After that would come his final expenses.

Charles took a sip of coffee. Best not to think on that. Not yet, anyway. For all he knew, he could wake up dead tomorrow.

"Pauline?"

The matronly waitress who had stopped to top off his mug looked up. "Yeah, Charles?"

"Would you bring me the deluxe patty melt…with fries?"

She scribbled on her pad. "Sure thing."

"And Pauline? You know what? I want a piece of chocolate cream pie, too."

She smiled, but she kept any wisecracks inside her head. "You got it."

The regular patty melt consisted of a single slice of cheddar oozing over a hamburger patty on pan-grilled rye bread. But the deluxe version came with a pickle, paper-thin slice of bacon, and what they advertised as a green salad. It was really just a small, sad bowl of iceberg lettuce that was most likely left over from the day before, topped with a pink cherry tomato. Or at least that's what he'd seen other patrons eating. He only ever ordered the basic patty melt, no extras, for himself. But all the scrimping had been worth it – he was the proud owner of a mostly new Cessna 140 airplane.

What had Orco had told him? He couldn't stop what was happening to him, no, too late for that. But perhaps he could slow down the process by being less greedy. What was the opposite of that? Being more generous? Something to think about.

Pauline set the warm plate - greasy sandwich nearly embedded in a stack of equally greasy fries. Charles inhaled deeply, trying to imprint the smell of the gooey cheese, grilled bread, beef drippings, and tang of the pickle onto his brain. He might need all of the pleasant memories he could capture in the near future. The waitress set down the salad (it looked as pathetic as any of the others he'd seen) and the pie. Oh, the pie! It was a glorious thing – tall chocolate custard piled high with sugared whipped cream and dusted with cocoa powder. Charles wondered if he should start with that.

13

Quetzel switched off the ignition and turned to Swann. "Don't get your hopes up. Homeless drunks don't often turn out to be reliable witnesses."

The Sobering Center stretched low and beige before them, and Quetzel wasn't feeling optimistic. Still, every lead had to be pursued, regardless of how flimsy.

The receptionist did not seem overly pleased to see them, but she had someone lead them to the employees' break room, where they would interview Robert Dudley, who claimed to have known the decedent.

A man in blue scrubs pushed a wheelchair into the room. "Here we are now, Mr. Dudley. The police are here to ask a few questions about what you saw." Robert slouched in the chair, curled into one side of it, his rheumy, yellow-stained eyes half open. He stank of the kind ground-in filth and hopelessness that never comes off, no matter how many hot showers one has.

"Hello, Mr. Dudley. I'm Sergeant Cazares. This is Detective Swann. How are you doing today?"

Dudley yawned. "Good. You here to take me to the HPD Hilton?"

"No, Mr. Dudley. We just want to ask you a few questions about what you said you saw in the park."

"The park?"

Swann sighed. Quetzel forced her voice to be even. "Yes, sir. You told the officers who brought you here that you knew the gentleman that was killed last night."

"Oh, yeah. Yeah. Trank. Trank wuddn't no gentleman, though."

"Trank's his nickname? You know his real name?"

"I only know what he tells me, and he tells me Trank." Dudley burped loudly.

Swann appeared unfazed, but Quetzel couldn't help coughing. *Ugh. You could strip paint with that dragon breath.* "Excuse me. Throat's a little dry. Do you know what happened to Trank?"

"Trank? He's dead. Yeah. Dead, dead, dead."

"Yes, sir. We know that. I just wondered if you'd seen anything that could help us find who killed him."

"It was a lobster."

Swann's jaw dropped. "A lobster? You're saying he was killed by a lobster?"

"Yep. He went off with some chick, then I looked up and he was fightin' a lobster. A big 'un, too."

Quetzel forced a polite smile. *Oh, well. At least it's a nice day to be out driving around.* "Did you happen to see what this woman looked like?"

"Nah. Wouldn't know her if I saw her. But she was pink."

"Pink. Okay. Is this someone he spent time with regularly?"

"Nah. Nah. Never seen her before."

Dudley scowled and turned his head.

"What's wrong, Mr. Dudley?" Quetzel asked.

"It's that damn lizard. Follows me everywhere I go. Don't you see it climbin' up the curtains?"

There was no lizard. At least not one Quetzel could see, anyway. "Well, thank you for your time, Mr. Dudley."

The nurse started to wheel Dudley out when he sat bolt upright. He looked at Swann. Just for a moment, his cloudy eyes were clear. He leaned forward, "You've got to find the rose."

"What rose?"

His eyes glazed over again. He collapsed back into his semi-fetal position. "Roses? I don't know nothin' 'bout no roses."

Swann squinted in the bright sun of the parking lot. "Well, that was a colossal waste of time."

Quetzel shrugged as she unlocked the doors. "You have to check everything." She thought the whole idea of Trank being attacked by a lobster was patently absurd. Still, she couldn't help hearing Cooper's voice in her head: '...*chitin is embedded in his bones.*'

Where is all this traffic coming from? It'll take all day to get out of the parking lot at this rate. "You got your phone handy, Swann? I want you to look something up for me, if you don't mind."

Swann retrieved the device from her bag and cleared the lock screen. "Ready."

"See what you can find out about chitin."

"Spell it?"

"C-h-i-t-i-n."

Swann browsed for the information. "Okay. It's a long-chain polymer derived from glucose, most commonly found in the exoskeletons of arthropods."

"Not sure that helps. Any industrial or medical uses for it?"

"Hold on." Swann read through a couple of sites. "Okay. Fertilizer, livestock food, water filtration, experimental uses, and paper making. Why, are you buying stocks or something?"

"Coop had called and told me that they'd found chitin on the raw bone ends of the corpses. I think industrial uses of the product are more of a clue than giant lobsters. But I could be wrong."

Swann tried to locate any storage and/or shipping facilities that dealt with chitin in the Houston area as they drove back downtown.

"No. You stay at the hospital with your wife, Tenner. I'm glad she's doing better. I'll cover for you, if anyone asks. Nothing's shaken loose yet." Her call waiting beeped. It was Bianca. Quetzel let it roll to voicemail.

"You need to go?"

Quetzel sighed. "It's Bianca."

"Oh. How's she?"

"Getting married."

"What? When?"

"This coming weekend."

"You never said anything."

"I just found out."

"Talk to your kid. I'll be in the office in the morning."

Quetzel decided to get a cup of coffee and a bag of pretzels before she returned the call.

"It took you long enough to call me back."

"I'm in the middle of a pretty major case. You might have heard about the South Loop Butcher on the news?"

"Whatever. I have details for the rehearsal dinner."

Quetzel wrote down the time and address.

"Make sure you wear something nice. And put on makeup. Also, could you pick up Justin's family at the airport?"

"Why can't Tawni-leigh do it?"

"She's getting her nails done then."

"Well, I suppose I could ask a patrol unit to swing by and get them. A lot of them have those new Tahoes that are pretty nice."

"You wouldn't."

"I don't have time. I'm under a lot of pressure –"

"Daddy said you would say 'no.'"

"If your father really wants to impress them, he should send a town car. Better yet, a limo."

"A limo? Good call, Mom."

Take that, Jorge's platinum Amex. "I've got to go. See you soon. Love you."

"Bye."

14

Nine years was a long time to live in the dark. Charles was tired. What Orco Mamman had told him was true – if he focused on being generous with things of the earth – for example, coins – the growth of the malignancy swallowing up his body slowed. Slowed, but didn't stop. He'd had to buy larger and larger hats to disguise the grotesque tumors on his head. His bones were beginning to warp and twist as the cancer took over. It hurt just to breathe. His mother begged him to go to a doctor. But what did Ebbie know? There wasn't any medicine that could cure what ailed him. Best save the money – he expected she'd need every penny he could squirrel away for her, because Fred's drinking had gotten worse over time.

The only place Charles had ever felt truly free was when he was flying. He loved that Cessna more than anything and took it up as often as he could, sometimes flying for days at a time over west Texas and down to Mexico. Perhaps it was slipping the surly bonds of Earth, as John Magee had so eloquently put it, that loosened the claws of Orco's curse just a little. The problem was,

planes were expensive, and his income had been halved.
It broke his heart to sell the plane after only three years,
but there was a meager consolation in having friends who
allowed him to fly their aircraft from time to time. But as
his disfigurement worsened, he did this less and less
often.

What Charles had taken up as both hobby and
mission was the futile attempt to save people from
themselves. Poor gamblers, specifically. The kind that his
old man preyed upon. Every payday, they'd come around,
betting more money than they could afford to lose on
Fred's back alley numbers games. Sure, some sucker
might get lucky and go home with money in his pocket,
but in the long run, the house always wins. The sweat and
blood that they'd converted to paychecks hardly stained
Fred's callous-free palms as he raked in far more cash
than he ever paid out.

He plucked the pigeons and handed most of the
feathers over to the local mob, what was left of them,
anyway. The major players - the Maceo brothers and
Jackie Freedman – had packed up and left for Vegas years
ago. Fred and his ilk were just vultures picking at the
moldering carcass of an enterprise long past its prime.
The old man had had to diversify into real estate scams to
keep himself in liquor. Even so, betting made a steady
income, and Fred had sticky fingers, so often a few extra
feathers stuck to his nest. But they didn't stay long – his
friends Jim, Jack, Johnnie, and José came too often to
party, and the old man closed himself in his room with
them until he was too stupefied to function.

Charles suspected that on some level, the desperate ones that threw their meager dollars like confetti at longshot lotteries knew they were being fleeced. But that craving for the big payoff overrode their better judgement. And this is where he came in.

All he had to do to clear the room was take off his hat. Of course, if the wise guys like his pop got wind of what he was doing, they'd put a bullet or six through his head without a second thought. He had to be careful, intercepting the sheep before they came to be sheared. It worked pretty well – fear is a stronger motivator than hunger. They'd be back again, he knew. But at least the rent might get paid and the kids might get fed before then.

The first time Charles ever felt afraid was in the summer of 1962.

He had heard about an icehouse on Shepherd Drive that was giving old Fred a run for his illegal gambling money, so he decided to see for himself. He parked around the corner and gave the partiers a little time to get good and plastered before he went in.

The place was hardly more than a large shed with an even larger patio. A few strings of naked bulbs crisscrossed the beer garden, held up by poles leaning at crazy angles, their anemic light barely reaching the well-worn picnic tables. A sunburnt awning covered about half the seating area, and a couple of dozen people milled around the yard and sat on the rough benches, city magpies flocking together for the evening.

Just as Charles opened his car door, the screaming started.

People came flooding out of the icehouse. Charles bucked the tide like a disoriented salmon, dodging panicked partygoers. He nearly got flattened by a man wind-milling his arms as if his crazy flailing would move his soft bulk any faster. Car doors slammed and gravel flew as dudes and chicks peeled out of the makeshift parking lot like bats out of Hell. *Did they all get a batch of electric hash? Looks like a major bad trip.*

All this background noise was washed out of focus by a single scream. Gutteral. Primal. Terror fused with agony, as it was torn from the depths of some poor soul, before fading – broken – into the dark. Hairs on the back of Charles' neck bristled and his blood turn to ice, freezing him in place just a few feet from the door.

Shadows moved behind a grimy window shade, showing a tragedy in silhouette. A tall figure - a man, Charles guessed – loomed over a smaller person, who, judging by the busty profile, was a woman. The man's arm extended toward the woman, but Charles couldn't tell if his hand rested on her shoulder or squeezed her throat. The other arm then rose stiffly from the man's side and pulled back the woman's head. He moved forward, as if to kiss her, but when his shadow bled into hers, her body convulsed and shuddered violently. Another arm reached out to steady the jerking body. And another.

What the hell? Four arms?

Charles heard a crunching sound, like a boot stepping on a cricket, only louder, wetter. The woman collapsed as if she were a marionette and her strings had suddenly been severed. Something rolled out the open door and stopped near his feet. Jeweled bobby pins in her hair glittered in the scant light that leaked from the shaded window. Dark splotches on her darker skin stank of hot blood. Black holes gaped where her eyes had been.

Charles ran. He didn't stop to puke until he got home.

He thought about calling the cops, but what would he tell them? Monsters were running loose in the city? They'd just think he was a crank.

When he finally tried sleeping, nightmares gnawed at his brain. Arms, too many arms, clasping his body and crushing his flesh.

Charles didn't leave his room the next night, or the one after that. Whether it was his parents' screaming at each other or his curiosity that got the better of him, he wasn't sure. He couldn't un-see that freakish shadow behind the window shade, or the head rolling out to stop at his feet. If people were getting chopped into bits, somebody had to know something about it.

He decided he may as well start with the bar on Shepherd.

He ordered whiskey, top shelf, neat. At this dive, though, their top and bottom shelf liquors were most likely the same thing

The shot was harsh as broken glass and burned all the way down. May as well have been industrial solvent. He didn't think his esophagus could stand another swallow of that nasty stuff. Charles thought it best to keep the glass next to him as a prop, however. Nothing would look more suspicious than a stranger in a bar without a drink.

If he got taken for a narc, these barflies would clam up in a New York minute.

He was careful to be subtle in scanning the room. Whoever had cleaned up the murder scene did a good job – no one who hadn't seen it would suspect what happened there three nights ago. Taking a moment to think about it, though, there had been surprisingly little blood. Head wounds bleed a lot, and decapitation is about as major a head would as anybody can get. He should have seen blood spraying everywhere, and the severed head should have been leaking like a torpedoed tanker. That was just one of the many things so very wrong with what he'd witnessed.

He forgot and almost took a sip of the rotgut. Covering, he only pretended to drink, but the whiff of it nearly made him gag. He never used to be a drinker, being on a first-name basis with the devil that lived in the bottle. But as his pain levels had increased, his objections had declined.

"Anybody sittin' here, hot stuff?"

Charles looked up. The woman who had her hand on the barstool next to him was no stone fox, that was for sure. But she wasn't a skank, either, and she might have a little info. Odds were, she was a working girl, and that was a point in her favor, information-wise.

"Looks like you are, darlin'." He gestured to the seat. "Buy you a drink?" Through practice, Charles had eradicated most of his Texas twang, but he let the remnants seep through now. He wanted to seem like just another working-class stiff, unremarkable and unmemorable.

As he half-stood to welcome his new companion, he reached out and knocked over the glass of whiskey. "Dammit!" he said, with mock chagrin.

The surly barkeep lumbered over with a dirty rag and mopped at the mess.

"Sorry," Charles said, although he wasn't the least bit sorry to be rid of the disgusting stuff. "What are you having?"

The lady shrugged. "A beer'll be fine."

"Two Pearls, please," he said to the barman.

The man grunted and turned away, heading toward the cooler.

"I'm Rick, by the way," Charles said. It wasn't exactly a lie – his middle name was Frederick.

"I'm Marilyn."

Charles eyed her nearly inch long dark roots and grinned as he nodded to her. *Of course you are.* "Pleased to make your acquaintance, Miss Marilyn."

"I ain't seen you around before. You from out of town?"

The barkeep returned with two bottles, condensation already beading up on them. Charles paid, and the man trundled off to the next customer.

"No, ma'am. I just live up the road a little bit. I work at night, so I don't get out too much."

"Well, I'm glad you ain't workin' tonight." She took a long slug from the beer bottle.

"Me, too, Marilyn. Me, too."

"Yeah. Had to check this place out." He looked around and leaned a little closer to her. "I heard somebody got shot here a couple of nights ago."

Marilyn's eyes widened and she pulled away. She and the bar tender exchanged glances. She put her hand over her mouth and coughed.

"I'm afraid I must be coming down with a cold, Rick. I should probably go home and lie down."

"Hope you feel better real soon, ma'am." He half rose as she got up and left.

Charles finished his beer, but he had apparently become invisible to the barman. They must think he's John Law. Something was going on here, but hanging around now wasn't going to help him find out what it was. He sauntered back out to his car.

A figure stood near it, a young girl. Betty. Lately she'd slipped out of his dreams and into his waking world more and more.

"Hey, sis."

She didn't reply, just gazed at him sadly for a few moments before she faded away.

Charles was running out of time.

15

Y ou look good, Babe."

Quetzel gave her ex a momentary stiff smile. Tawni-leigh stared flaming spears at her.

"What do you want, Jorge?" Quetzel rearranged her silverware.

Putting his hand across his chest, Jorge said, "I'm shocked. And a little hurt. I can't pay the mother of my beautiful daughter a compliment without being accused of ulterior motives?"

Tawni-leigh, sandwiched between Jorge and Justin, inched closer to her husband and made a show of resting her hand on Jorge's inner thigh.

Any other day, I get texts and phone calls from work at dinner time. But not today. Why not today? The detective crossed her ankles under her chair and straightened her posture the final millimeter or two she had left before her spine was at exactly 90° to the chair. "Jorge, this is Bianca's rehearsal dinner. Could we skip the drama, please?"

"I'm just trying to be nice to you, and you give me attitude, but I'm the one bringing the drama?" Jorge's voice was loud enough that other diners turned to watch the show. "Maybe you are the one who needs to take a closer look at yourself, maybe talk to somebody about your need to make everybody else look bad."

How many years of marriage had it taken Quetzel to learn that you can't reason with a narcissist? Years of being built up, then torn down had left her with little tolerance for his manipulations.

"Fine. Jorge. Thank you. Thank you for the lovely compliment. Oh, look. Here's the server with the soup. I'm sure that the expensive food that you've paid for will be very, very delicious. Why don't we all enjoy it now, and bask in its expensive deliciousness?" She finished with a broad, fake smile that, on reflection, probably made her look insane.

There was an awkward silence as Justin's family tried to figure out which side to choose.

"Well, I completely agree with Bianca's mom," Justin's older sister said. "This soup smells heavenly."

The waiter distributed trendy square bowls of steaming soup around the table.

"What kind of soup is this, again?" Justin's father asked.

"Turtle soup, sir."

"Ah! The famous turtle soup. Jorge knows how to pick a winner."

Jorge, of course, smiled broadly. Silver spoons clinked against china.

Quetzel reached for the bread plate. She hadn't gone full vegetarian – she still ate seafood, and occasionally chicken, but red meat on a plate didn't look all that different from what she saw at just about every crime scene. Ground bits of turtle, floating in the broth, reminded her of Fred and Ebbie Rogers, stacked neatly in their own refrigerator like so much future dinner. But even without this train of thought, spicy food irritated her ulcer, and just having the soup in front of her made her eyes water from the cayenne wafting off it.

"Look, Bianca." Jorge looked at his daughter with a pained expression. "Your mother is not eating her soup." He frowned and sighed loudly. "I thought we were here to celebrate, but she won't even break bread with the rest of us. So sad that she'd put her petty grievances above her family." He shook his head.

Quetzel picked up the buttered slice of bread on her plate. "The soup is spicy. I forgot to take my Zantac. Sorry." *But you know I can't eat spicy things, which I assume is why you chose a Cajun-Creole restaurant.*

Bianca squirmed. Justin rubbed her shoulder. A scowl flickered across Tawni-leigh's face and she shifted herself in her chair so that she was no longer draped over her husband.

Cooper Morgenstern, please call me. Now. About anything. Just get me out of here. Quetzel kept her fake smile plastered on her mouth, even as she chewed the sourdough bread with its elegant gourmet butter. If Jorge was calling her out over the soup, she didn't want to be there when the blackened red snapper showed up.

The cell phone chimed just as Quetzel reached for her iced tea. It wasn't Cooper Morgenstern. It was dispatch.

"Cazares." Quetzel pulled her notebook from her bag. "Got another one."

Quetzel wrote down the address. "On my way." *Sad that this is a better deal than my daughter's rehearsal dinner.*

"I'm so sorry, Bianca. I really have to go. It's been nice meeting all of you." She looked at Justin's parents.

"Why do you have to leave?" Justin's mother whined. She seemed like the type who was always on the lookout for reasons to be offended.

"Death scene investigation. Enjoy your soup."

Quetzel had talked with a lot of murderers. More often than not, deaths were from fights over sex or money. Drug dealer turf wars. Infidelity. Inheritance. Crimes committed by ordinary people with poor impulse control.

But serial killers were a whole 'nother animal. They had their own twisted reasons for doing what they did. She had watched interviews with Ted Bundy. When he talked about the killings, he referred to himself in the third person, and said about how a dark force took control of his actions. The-Devil-Made-Me-Do-It excuse had been around as long as people have been committing crimes, and the detective didn't buy into it. Some people were just wired wrong.

But as she looked down at this corpse, she almost reconsidered. If there was such a thing as a demonic killer, this was his handiwork. It was nearly dark, and the glare of the portable floodlight made each stark detail that much more obvious.

The head had been found by a couple out jogging. It hadn't been recognizable as a human head – it was only when their dog tried to pick it up and rolled it around that the bloody, vacant eye sockets above a broken nose and slashed lips revealed what it truly was. Further off the path, partially hidden by shrubbery, lay the heap of limbs and torso - the fragmented remains of the corpse. Cleaned, drained of blood.

The first body's arms had been disarticulated at the elbow. The next three had not. Had the killer run out of time, or just gotten tired of sawing?

Out of the corner of her eye, Quetzel saw her rookie detective approaching.

"Sorry I'm late. I was in the shower at the gym when the call dropped."

Reflexively, Cazares reached into her bag and retrieved a small jar of mentholated salve.

"You've got to remember to pack one of these for death scenes. Especially ones outside in the heat."

"Thanks, but I don't need it, remember?" Swann tapped her nose. "What makes people do something like this?" She shook her head.

"Excellent question," a male voice behind them answered.

Quetzel turned and appraised the newcomer. Dark suit. White shirt. Clean cut and trim. Squinting under the floodlights. "You must be the FBI guy."

He smiled. "That's me. Agent Cadence Mitchell, with the BAU."

Cazares reached out and flipped his ID around – the lanyard had become twisted and the back was showing. It looked like all the other FBI tags she'd seen, although a smudge of what appeared to be cream cheese partially obscured the photo. "I'm Sergeant Cazares. This is Detective Swann. We're the primaries, although" she glanced around at the swarm of investigators, "we've been getting lots of help."

"Yes. That's why I'm here." He smiled, more a punctuation than an emotion.

You look awfully young for a behavioral analyst. "Have you had a briefing?"

"I reviewed the case files on the flight over from Langley. But perhaps you could refresh my memory. This is the fourth DB, but when was the first found, again?"

"That's a good question."

"What?" Swann seemed surprised.

"We started finding dismembered bodies three weeks ago, same general area. This gentleman is number five. However, I have a cold case on my desk with the same MO from 1965. There are others that go as far back as 1959. Don't know if they're connected though."

"Really?" Mitchell said. "Must be a copycat – dismembering a body is difficult work – I can't see an old person being able to carry that out. 1965 was over fifty years ago. Have you ever heard of a seventy-five year-old serial killer, Detective?" His smirk oozed from his voice onto his thin lips.

Quetzel clenched her jaw and forced a smile. "You might be surprised at the things I've heard of. Experience is funny that way. I'm sure the Copeland Farm rings a bell?"

His eyes narrowed for an instant – a micro expression – but it didn't escape Quetzel's notice. "Not familiar with that one."

You should know this, coming from BAU.

"What are you talking about?" Swann broke in.

"Oklahoma, 1989. Farmer Ray Copeland paid a series of drifters to help him out in a cattle-buying fraud scheme, then he took them out behind the farmhouse and shot them. His wife, Faye, made a quilt from scraps of their clothes. The couple was in their 70s. Although, I'm not entirely convinced that Ray Copeland was a classic serial killer – he was simply getting rid of witnesses." *That case is older that either one of you.*

"Charming." Swann shook her head, but Quetzel noticed the quick once-over she gave Agent Mitchell.

"Did you bring gloves?" Quetzel handed Mitchell a pair of purple nitrile gloves from her bag before he could answer.

"Thanks," he said, taking them. "I didn't realize I would be coming straight from the airport to a crime scene."

"We don't waste any time here in H-Town."

Swann rolled her eyes. "Yeah. Except when you're on the Loop, any time of day, going two miles an hour."

Agent Mitchell smiled, perhaps a little too broadly.

Clearing her throat, Cazares stepped aside. "All right, Mr. Behavioral Analysis. I've got four more in the freezer just like this. What do you make of our killer?"

Mitchell walked around the pile of body parts, before finding a place to squat and examine them more closely. "Has this already been photographed?"

"Yes."

The corpse's left hand and arm lay on top of the stack. Mitchell reached for it, rotating it around to examine the severed end. "I would say it's an organized killer. Decedent was clearly murdered somewhere else and dumped here."

"Why do you say that?" Swann asked.

Quetzel looked heavenward. Basic stuff like this was part of her training.

"No blood, for one thing. No evidence of a struggle – even if it was an ambush, there would be blood spatter, given the condition of the head."

"Anything else?" Cazares asked.

"I'll be able to complete my analysis after I get a copy of the coroner's report."

"I see." Mitchell's credentials looked real, but Quetzel doubted he was from the BAU. He couldn't tell her any more that what someone who'd ever watched a single episode of any given true crime show could have come up with. Surely the Bureau hadn't let their standards slip that much.

"Alright, Detective Swann, I don't think there's much more we can do out here. Why don't we get out of the Crime Scene Unit's way?" Quetzel started toward the taped-off perimeter, peeling off her gloves.

Mitchell grinned, following her, also stripping off the nitrile. "What's your pet theory?"

"Oh! Dammit!" Swann stumbled and her cell phone skittered across the grass to Mitchell's feet.

"You okay?" He handed her the device and reached out to steady her.

"Sorry. Don't know what's gotten into me today. I've tripped over my own shadow twice already." She raised the phone. "Thanks."

Honey, we're going to have to talk. "Can we give you a lift, Agent Mitchell?"

Cadence opened his mouth, as if to say 'yes,' then stopped himself. He gestured randomly to his left. "I have a rental."

"We'll see you back at Travis, then."

"On my way." Mitchell turned towards the parked cars.

"Hold up a sec." Swann strode after him. "You forgot something."

Quetzel noticed she had her cuffs concealed in one hand. She also moved toward Mitchell. Clearly, Swann knew something that she didn't.

Before the agent knew what was happening, Swann had snapped a handcuff onto his right wrist. He tried to spin away and chicken-wing his left arm up and away from her, but Quetzel grabbed his elbow and rotated his arm backward. He struggled to pull the limb away from her, but she put a foot in the back of his knee and he went to the ground. "Stop resisting. You're making it worse."

Swann finished cuffing him. "Stay down."

By this time, other officers were running to assist. He wasn't going anywhere.

"What's going on?" Mitchell's voice cracked. "This is outrageous."

"I went to Sam with Cadence Mitchell. You're not him."

"I'm not saying anything until I talk to my lawyer."

16

Charles thought the coyotes sounded more like hyenas than wolves. He could relate to whatever they were chasing – probably a jackrabbit – as the frenzied yipping rolled through the hunting pack. They were uncomfortably close, and he shivered, even as he stood sweating at the wooded edge of a field at the ass-end of nowhere. He was being swallowed up, eaten alive, by Orco's curse.

He sincerely hoped he didn't have to run for it, because if he did, he was toast. His skin had stiffened and taken on a rough texture that reminded him of shale, but less brittle. It was difficult to walk, and the only thing that hurt as much as moving was being still. While the oil seeps had largely stopped, his rocky hide now warped into escarpments and fissures. Charles had taken to wearing a trench coat to hide the grotesque geography of his body. To him, it felt like a funeral shroud. To others, while it would have been unremarkable in January, it must have seemed downright peculiar in June. Currently, however, he and his cousin, Raymond, were both dressed in ghillie suits. Perhaps Raymond's vision was better than his, but Charles couldn't locate his cousin unless he moved. He hoped he was just as invisible.

Two years had passed since he'd witnessed the murder at the ice house. The woman had been a prostitute. Nobody knew her real name, but her street name was 'Honey.' Nothing but her skull had been found months after her death, prompting a paragraph or so write-up in the back of the paper.

Ferreting out details regarding her murder had been difficult. In a sudden lust for respectability, city governments had cracked down on vice, and driven the drug dealers, gamblers, and hookers underground. This had made the pimps extra wary, and they wouldn't think twice about putting the hurt on anybody looking into their business. Swimming with the gators in Buffalo Bayou wasn't out of the question.

One thing Charles did know, however, was that Honey wasn't the first, or even the second, at least partially dismembered corpse to turn up lately. He'd scoured the newspapers, sometimes even driving out of town to get a copy of non-local rag. So far, eight others had been found, starting in 1959, scattered (as it were) mostly across Texas and New Mexico. Body parts were also found in Florida, Ohio, and Georgia. Of those victims, only one had been identified. Charles was aware of this sinister trend because he had been looking for it. The details were all similar – no blood; in all cases but one, no head; legs disarticulated at either the knee or hip; hands severed at the wrists; and arms removed at either elbows or shoulders. While he couldn't prove that these cases were connected, dismemberment was uncommon.

There were rumors, of course, of a shadowy crime boss who specialized in drugs and whores. He didn't tolerate failure or betrayal. In that line of work, a retirement plan tended to include a free pair of cement overshoes. Or in this case, seemingly, a surgical plan. It had taken time to find the right hangouts and eavesdrop on the right people, because nobody was going to tell a stranger anything. They spoke in codes and generalities, and Charles had to piece together what he heard, hoping he hadn't guessed wrong. His bygone days in Naval Intelligence served him well now.

Raymond, turned out to be invaluable, too. Although they'd grown up together, Charles hadn't seen much of him as an adult. Ray had spent most of his young adult years in and out of the joint. He was out, at least for now, and he knew the best places to find the worst people.

And this is how Charles and Raymond came to be standing in the shadows of the trees that outlined a hayfield that ran along Jones Creek, wearing hot, itchy camouflage suits. An ex-con who'd shared a cell with Raymond told him that another guy he'd done time with organized parties. The venue was only the classiest – under the bridge where Farm to Market Road 359 crossed Jones Creek. It was out in the boondocks for sure, but the party favors included psilocybin, pot, and party girls. Dearly departed Honey used to be a regular participant in the festivities. The area was all but deserted, but people fished in the creek near that bridge from time to time, so a couple of cars on the side of the road meant nothing to any of the local yokels who happened by. And if they had cash, they were welcome to join the party.

Raymond swatted at a mosquito. "Ain't nothin' gonna happen, cuz."

"Still early. The girls haven't even shown up yet. It's only been dark for an hour." Charles leaned over to retrieve the infrared night vision scope he'd gotten from the army surplus store. He struggled to bend far enough to heft the gadget from the ground. Raymond grunted as he picked it up and handed it to his cousin.

"Thanks."

Raymond nodded.

The starlight wasn't as bright as he needed it to be, but his task wasn't difficult. At least it wouldn't be, if these ghillie suit flaps and filaments didn't keep getting in his way. Charles set up the scope, which weighed almost ten pounds, resting it on a low tree limb. Ten pounds didn't sound like a lot, but trying to hold it steady and look through the clunky thing was not easy. It was designed to be attached to a carbine rifle, and the 'hand-held' option was more of an afterthought than a deliberate design. They'd come up earlier in the day and scouted a location. FM 359 swept sharply to the north just past the bridge, and they'd concealed Charles' motorcycle in the bushes there.

The sidecar had been a new experience, and Charles hated the feeling of not being in control. But there wasn't a damn thing he could do about it, so he had closed his eyes and hoped Raymond didn't run the bike into a ditch. Charles could no longer move fast enough to control the motorcycle, not unless they were going down a long, stick-straight road with no traffic or stop lights. As much as Charles was grateful that his cousin helped him out, he resented his dependency on him.

"You got that thing working yet, Charles?"

With the flip of a switch, the power supply hummed softly. "I think so."

"I don't see nothin'."

"You aren't supposed to. It's infrared."

"Well, what's the point of that?"

Charles waved him over. "Look through here." He tapped the scope.

"Hot damn!" In his exuberance, Raymond tried to swivel the scope around and knocked it off the limb.

"Shhh! They aren't that far away." Charles groped in the tall grass to find the device, then re-positioned it. A half-dozen or so grey and black figures moved in the small circle of the sniper scope, milling around under the bridge with cans of what was most likely beer. They were at the outer edge of the scope's range of a little more than a hundred yards.

He couldn't see the far side of the bridge with the scope, but he did see a light moving down the side of the road. Looked like either a flashlight or a lantern. The pale orb disappeared momentarily behind the bridge, then reappeared underneath it. It was accompanied by three ladies, all wearing mini-skirts and probably go-go boots, and two men. The beer drinkers swarmed around them.

One of the new male arrivals towered over everyone else. It was hard to tell without knowing how tall the other people were, but Charles guessed his height at about 6'6". There was something not right about the tall man. Perhaps it was just the distance and the dim light, but to Charles' eye, his movement was off, as if there were extra joints in his spine. This freakishness cast a pall of unease over him.

"Have a look at this, Ray."

His cousin put is eye to the scope. "Day-um. That is a big ole boy, I tell you what."

"You notice anything else about him?"

"Nah. But I bet that's some fine poon-tang down there."

Charles rolled his eyes in the dark. Raymond's taste in women had always been questionable at best. "Yeah, sure."

The first pungent whiff of marijuana smoke had made its way to their hiding spot. Charles scowled. He didn't want his senses to be compromised by the drug, should the breeze keep blowing it in their direction. "What's the big guy doing?"

"Looks like he's mad at Denny." Raymond chortled unpleasantly.

Charles elbowed him away from the scope.

The tall man gestured at two of the women, who stood apart from the rest. Denny raised his hands in supplication. The two ladies moved back into the small group, and the argument appeared to be over.

"What's going on?" Ray asked, petulant.

"Be still! If they see us, they aren't going to invite us to the party."

Ray huffed just loudly enough for Charles to hear him. After a few minutes, he said. "You could at least let me have another look."

Not much was happening. Charles took a breath. He opened his mouth to say, 'Fine. Have a quick look.'

But that's not what came out.

"Oh, hell."

"What? What's happening?"

"Get down Ray! Don't move. Don't make a sound."

"But —"

"Now!"

Charles couldn't pry his eyes from the sniper scope. Denny, the party organizer, cowered against one of the concrete bridge supports, while Mr. Big loomed over him. Denny put his hands up, as if to protect his face. Although he was too far away for Charles and Ray to hear the conversation, his scream was loud and clear. Eerily similar in raw terror to the one Charles had heard coming from Honey the night he watched her murder in the ice house.

The bridge people fled, running pell-mell and knocking each other down in their panic to get back to their cars.

The tall man stood with his back to Charles. But he was different. Now he was eight? Nine? Feet tall.

And no longer human.

Instead of clothing, his back was covered in bony plates. And legs! There were legs and snapping claws everywhere, as if the creature was the result of some unholy union between a spider and a lobster.

Denny tried to run with the rest, but the monstrous thing snagged him with a clawed appendage.

Good god! How many legs does this thing have?

The creature's back was still toward him, and he could only see Denny's limbs, flailing wildly as he was lifted off the ground. A howl from Denny was cut short and he went limp. Moments later, his body fell to the ground in pieces.

Slowly, the bug turned, staring right at Charles' hiding spot. He could feel it looking at him.

Oh, fuck. It can see the infrared.

Charles knocked the scope to the ground, his fingers clawing for the off button.

"What's happening? Ray asked, his voice a broken whisper.

"Shh! Be still"

Ray didn't move, but Charles could hear the grass shivering around him.

The horror that had been a man came closer, blotting out the stars as it loomed larger.

Charles swallowed. He and Raymond were going to die.

A loud tractor engine grumbled from the other side of the field and two dull yellow lights shuddered over the bumpy terrain. The vehicle came to a stop about halfway between the tree line and the bridge, and the growl quieted to a purr.

The double clack of a pump action shotgun was unmistakable.

"Get off my land! Damn Hippies! How many times I have to tell you don't come around here?"

The monstrous creature, outside the reach of the dim beams, seemed to consider its options, then retreated. Charles and Ray lay frozen in the grass like two petrified rabbits. The tractor did not leave until a car door slammed in the distance. Headlights came on, and an engine revved. Tires squealed on pavement, and red tail lights disappeared around the curve.

The tractor turned, sweeping by the trees and missing Ray's foot my less than a yard. It had been gone for long minutes before Charles lifted his head to look around. Crickets chirped as if nothing had happened.

The coyotes started to sing again. They were closer this time. He wondered how much of Denny would be left in the morning.

17

The man claiming to be FBI Agent Cadence Mitchell was loaded into the back of a police cruiser and taken downtown. At the very least, he could be charged with impersonating a peace officer and resisting arrest.

"Wouldn't that be something if the South Loop Butcher just wrapped himself up in a tidy little package and hand delivered it to us? Too bad he didn't have any real ID on him."

"Well, I might have his prints." Still wearing her gloves, Swann raised her phone.

Quetzel grinned. "Clever girl." She took out an evidence bag and held it up. "If we hand-deliver it to the lab, we might be able to get a jump on his booking prints."

Swann dropped the phone in. "Like I said, Cadence Mitchell was in my graduating class at Sam Houston State. He's about 6'4". Thought it was possible that they just happened to have the same uncommon name, but when he said he'd come from Langley, I knew he was a fake. Everybody knows Behavioral Analysis is out of

Quantico." She leaned over and picked up Mitchell's discarded gloves from the top of the trash can and put them in another bag.

"If this guy is our killer, and you tricked him into leaving his finger prints and possibly DNA evidence behind, you will be a legend."

Swann blushed slightly and looked down. "Why would the killer show up at the crime scene pretending to be an FBI agent? That makes no sense."

"It's not uncommon for murderers to try and 'help' the investigation so that they can see how much we know. Some killers get off on taunting the cops. At least this one hasn't written any letters to newspapers blaming his neighbor's demon-possessed talking dog."

"Not yet, anyway. But if it turns up, it'll be on YouTube, not the papers." Swann sealed up the evidence bag.

Quetzel handed her a marker to fill out the form printed on the sacks. "Let's go see what the lab can find."

The forensics lab director was only too happy to prioritize this particular fingerprint search. There was a hit almost immediately. It was verified as a match to one Philip Nolan, a YouTuber who had more than one BE to his credit. He had been thoughtful enough to record his breaking and entering activities and broadcast them on his channel as part of his video blog, so his convictions were no-brainers. BE, on its own, is a misdemeanor, and he'd filmed himself grinning as he paid his fines in cash, claiming *The Peoples' Investigator* wins again. Quetzel had watched the videos soon after Nolan had been identified, and they started combing through his social media. He'd also made uploads mocking the investigation into the South Loop Butcher.

Philip Nolan's lawyer had quit when his client had phoned him, and now the wanna-be internet personality sat sniveling in the interrogation room. Quetzel wanted him to have time to stew in his own juices before she questioned about the murders.

She and Swann headed north to visit Nolan's residence – it was almost to the airport. The apartment looked like she'd expected for a college-aged, single male – pizza boxes on the coffee table, half-drunk soda bottles perched on every corner, and dirty clothes on the floor. But there were no obvious signs of murder and mayhem. There wasn't even a bathtub in the studio apartment, just a tiny shower tucked into one corner of the bathroom. If Philip Nolan had chopped up bodies, he almost certainly hadn't done it there. South Loop Butcher or no, there was jail time involved for impersonating an FBI agent. The *NoLaN PI* channel would be waiting a while for its next upload.

"There you are!"

Quetzel looked over her shoulder toward the outburst. A decidedly scruffy man who towered over the officer at the door had just been let in.

"Hello, Amanda." He grinned at Swann.

"Hey, Cade. Glad it's really you this time."

"Yep. The one and only." He pivoted and put out his hand. "You must be Sergeant Cazares. Cadence Mitchell. I've heard a lot about you."

His dark hair was frosted with grey and the stubble on his chin was more salt than pepper. She looked at Swann and back to Mitchell. "I'm sorry." She shook his hand. "When Swann told me that she'd gone to college with you, I expected-"

"Someone a lot younger?" He chuckled. "I was a clinical psychologist before I decided on a career change and went back to school."

"Yeah." Quetzel took in his unusual eyes – they were both blue, but his left eye had a sector, perhaps as much as a third of the iris, that was brown. She shook herself. "So, what do you think, Agent Mitchell? Do these look like a serial killer's digs to you?"

"Too early to tell. So far, no body parts laying around, though." He winked.

Quetzel nodded absently. "How did this blogger end up with your ID? He doesn't exactly seem to be a criminal mastermind."

"I was in the bathroom at the airport, and a kid ran in and swiped my carry-on when…my hands were full."

The question of just how full flickered across Quetzel's mind and she chided herself for being foolish.

The most objectionable things found in Philip Nolan's apartment had been a moldy half-eaten bowl of cereal under his bed, a partially smoked blunt in his underwear drawer, and a past-due credit card bill. The computer guys had taken his laptop and a handful of USB drives back to the lab earlier, but they hadn't found anything yet. Mitchell waited in the observation room. Cazares and Swann entered the interrogation room.

Quetzel's nose wrinkled for a second. *Great. He's peed himself.* "I'm Sergeant Cazares and this is Detective Swann. You may remember us from the crime scene earlier."

"I remember." Nolan's voice shook.

"Would you like to tell us why you were impersonating a peace officer during a criminal investigation?"

"It was for my show." Nolan was sullen. "Now Imma be way off schedule."

Swann broke in, "Would you like a coke or something Mr. Nolan?"

"A Sprite." He licked his lips. "Please?"

"I'll be right back."

When the door clicked shut behind Swann, Quetzel propped both elbows up on the table and interlaced her fingers. "I'm very curious to know, Phil – may I call you Phil?" He didn't respond, so she continued. "I'd like to know how you came to be in possession of Agent Mitchell's official identification."

"That. That was all luck. One hundred percent. I was taking the trash out to the dumpster at my apartments when I saw this suitcase. You know, one of them rolley bags. It was out by the trash, so I figured it was fair game. Looked brand new, so I took it in with me."

"That is an amazing coincidence. You finding a carry-on stolen from an FBI agent, then showing up at a crime scene, pretending to be that agent. He didn't even know about the murder – he was in the air when it was discovered. How is it that you knew where to come?"

Nolan's mouth gaped open, then shut. "It-it was on the police scanner app on my phone."

"Oh, Phil. You know as well as I do that any radio chatter about the South Loop Butcher is going to happen over a secure channel."

Nolan went pale. "You don't think I-I had anything to do with this!"

"What should I think, Phil? You record these videos making fun of the police – that's hurtful, Phil. Hurtful. You miraculously recover the stolen luggage of an FBI behavioral analyst sent out to help find the killer, and then you turn up at a crime scene which wasn't public knowledge. If you were me, what would you think?"

Nolan started to sob, an ugly, wet sound. "Please. I didn't do anything. At least, I didn't kill nobody. I found the suitcase, swear to God, by the dumpster. My friend, Eli, he's got a tool to hack the radio. We heard about the fifth body. I thought…I thought I could get the dope on these murders, 'cuz y'all ain't gettin' the job done. I didn't hurt nobody."

The door opened, and Swann returned with the soda. She opened it for him, and handed him a box of tissues. "Are you alright?"

"Yes," he sniffled.

The text chime on Quetzel's phone went off. It was a message from Detective Ilyn: "Got security footage you need to see ASAP."

18

The past year had not been kind to Charles. He felt he was turning to stone, a living, (barely) breathing fossil. His skin was tough, but it still bled. His joints creaked and groaned, but they still moved, just not very much. He spent most of his time downstairs on the living room couch. He could struggle up the stairs to his tiny attic room, but he was breathless and gasping when he got to the landing. Ebbie fretted over him, but he wasn't sure if her concern was more for his health or her furniture.

Raymond didn't bother knocking any more. He came in the side door and hung Charles' dry cleaning on the coat rack.

Charles looked at the khaki trench coat. The hem had started to fray, and he didn't know why he even bothered having it cleaned and pressed any more. He hadn't left the house in weeks.

Ray grinned. "Friday night. Was thinking I'd go out. Maybe see a picture show."

"You have a date?" Charles rasped.

"Maybe."

"Knock yourself out."

Raymond smiled softly. He refilled Charles' water glass and made him a peanut butter sandwich. "Right. I'm headed out"

"Have fun."

He sighed when the screen door slapped against the doorframe and Raymond was gone. It was only a matter of time before Ebbie came home from her part time job at the grocery store and she and Fred would be at each other's throats.

Charles was so tired. Living with pain was exhausting, and he had to struggle for each breath. It wouldn't be long now, though. He could feel it.

Day after tomorrow would be Father's Day. Maybe he would send Ray down to Weingarten's for a card in the morning. If he thought about it. Probably not, though.

The window behind him gaped open, and he watched the patch of light on the wall in front of him fade from grey to black. Fred's bedroom door opened and he stumbled out, clumsy in his stupor. Charles could smell the reek of whiskey and stale sweat across the room.

He glared at his son. "You shtill here?" His words slurred together.

"Yeah, Pop. Still here."

Fred grunted, then made his way out the front door. Charles heard the bushes around the front door shake before his father's uneven steps faded into the evening.

Ten o'clock had come and gone before his mother returned.

"I had a sales meeting," she said, by way of apology.

Charles nodded. She seemed to have lots of Stanley Home Products sales meetings, but never got around to actually selling any of the inventory that collected dust in the kitchen.

"Fred went out."

Ebbie's shoulders relaxed. "Would you like me to put on some coffee?"

"It's late, Ma. No thanks. Raymond brought me a glass of water, but I could use a top-up."

"Sure. Sure." She glanced around the living room. "Is he still around?"

"He had a date."

"I see." Her eyes widened. "Have you had anything to eat today?"

"Ray made me a sandwich. I'm good. Thanks, though." It took surprisingly little to fill him up these days.

Ebbie bit her lip. "Bless him. I was worried when he started hanging around. Didn't want him to steal any of my valuables, since he just got out of prison."

You don't have any valuables, Ebbie.

"But he's been a real godsend, helping take care of you and all."

She took a step toward him and reached out her hand to touch him. But she pulled back, as if his cursed skin might be contagious.

"I'm tired as a dog. Good night, Charles."

"Good night, Ma."

It was almost lunchtime on Saturday, and Fred had
yet to return.

"You think he's coming back?" Hope tinged the edges
of Ebbie's voice.

Charles made his best effort at a shrug. His shoulders
were barely mobile, and a large outcropping from the top
of his ribcage forced him to carry his left arm at an
awkward angle.

"You know Fred. He always seems to come out
smelling like a rose, when by rights, he should be pushing
up daisies. It's almost like he's made a deal with the
Devil."

"Don't say such things! It's bad luck to invite him into
your house."

"Who, Fred?"

Ebbie smiled, just a little. "You know what I mean."

"You could leave him, you know."

"I'm an old lady, Charles. At seventy-nine, it's too late
to make such a change."

"I own the house, remember? You'd have a place to
stay."

Charles knew she would never go through with it.
She'd tried leaving Fred more than once, but couldn't
keep herself away from his dubious charms.

The side door creaked, and both Ebbie and Charles
caught their breaths.

"Hey," said Raymond, giving them a quizzical look.

Charles sighed inwardly with relief. "How was the
picture show?"

"Picture show?" Ray fidgeted with something in his
pocket.

"You know, your date?"

"Oh, yeah. That. It was good. It was the airplane race one. With Red Skeleton."

"Skelton," Ebbie corrected.

"Yeah. Him."

"Ray, I need your help with something. Can you go find that keyhole saw in the garage and meet me upstairs?"

"If you boys have work to do, I'll go and tidy the kitchen."

Eisenhower was president last time you *tidied the kitchen.*

Charles dragged himself up the stairs and into his attic room, collapsing on the bed. Ray was taking his sweet time, but he'd probably stopped for a cigarette break. It was okay – gave Charles a chance to recover. Finally, Raymond's steps thudded on the steps. The door to Charles' room opened soundlessly.

"Close the door. I don't want Ma to see."

"See what?"

Charles lifted his arm and pulled his shirt tight against his ribs. "See this bump? I want you to cut it off."

"What? No."

"It isn't…going to hurt. Probably won't even bleed. Not much, anyway. Please. I'd do it myself, if I could. But this thing makes it almost impossible to use my arm. I'm already – There's already so much I can't do. I really need your help. Please, Ray?"

"Oh, no. Aunt Ebbie'd kill me if I got blood all over her house."

Charles seized the saw and, with a somewhat less than fluid motion, dragged the blade across his forearm. Raymond gasped. A thin red line appeared along the saw's path. Hardly enough blood welled up to form a droplet, much less make a mess.

Raymond sighed heavily and took the saw. "Fine."

"I need help with my shirt."

Ray pulled the offending garment over his cousin's head, perhaps a bit too roughly. Charles tried to raise his arm, but couldn't get it as high as shoulder level. Raymond didn't have access to the bulge.

"I have an idea." Charles said.

"What's that, cuz?"

"I'm going to sit on the bed and prop my arm on the dresser."

Ray helped his cousin maneuver into place. "Not quite high enough."

"Why don't you run downstairs and get a can of soup or something?"

"What kind of soup?"

"What? It doesn't matter. We only care about the can."

"Oh."

Ray left the room and Charles heard the rapid clonk-clonk-clonk his boots made on the wood stairs. It was too much work to move into a more comfortable position, so Charles sat where he was.

Only a few minutes passed before Raymond returned with a large can of stewed tomatoes.

"You're sure about this, Charles?"

"Yeah. Come on. Let's get it done."

After a little hesitation, Ray tried to work the can underneath Charles' arm. Groaning with the effort, Charles rose from the bed a few inches to allow a little clearance. It worked, and now his arm was levered up just above shoulder level. It didn't hurt, exactly, but it was far from comfortable.

"I'm not sure I can do this." The saw wavered in Ray's hand.

"I would do it myself, if I could reach. I really need your help here, Ray."

Ray squeezed his eyes almost shut and moved closer. Charles could feel the disgust in his cousin's fingertips as he felt around the baseball-sized lump to place the saw.

The jagged blade rasped across Charles' skin, and he gasped. "Stop!"

Ray almost jumped across the room.

It hurt much more than Charles had expected. A small amount of blood – perhaps a teaspoon – smeared the keyhole blade. "Alright," he panted, "that's not going to work. Can you help me downstairs?"

Ray picked up Charles' shirt and slipped it over his cousin's stiff arms. He'd only gotten the first three buttons done.

"That's good enough."

"What about the saw?"

"Worry about it later. Just please help me downstairs *now*. I have to piss like a Russian race horse."

"You ain't had to tell me that." Ray helped tug Charles' arms down as near to his sides as they got these days. He couldn't quite hold the stair railing, and he doubted he could catch himself if he fell. That's why Raymond walked two steps below him. Charles' uneven gait caused him to lurch against the railing with every other step, leaving little smears of blood from his aborted surgery behind him.

His sister stood waiting at the bottom of the stairs, shaking her head but smiling. "That was a silly thing to do, Charlie-Boy."

"Yeah, probably."

"What?" Ray asked.

"Nothing. Just thinking out loud."

Now that Betty was talking to him, instead of merely lurking and staring, he knew that his time was short.

Fred did not return home until noon on Sunday. It wasn't unusual for him to disappear for days on end, but it hadn't happened much since he crossed the octogenarian threshold. Charles heard him coming up the walkway, arguing with someone. Ebbie had started to relax a little in his absence, but curled into herself like a beaten dog at the sound of his voice. Raymond, who'd been lazing in the armchair with the newspaper and a cold bottle of beer, sat up and looked toward the side door. Charles expected he was making a calculation on whether or not he had time to make a run for it.

The front door clicked open.

"You're crazy!" Fred shouted. "That's not my bag – I don't run whores or drugs, neither one."

"Then where's the money gone, old man? Jimmy said he'd dropped almost a grand in your lottery game, but you showed up with less than two hundred."

"Eh! What does Jimmy know about numbers? He wasn't the only one playing, and he wasn't there all night."

Charles couldn't see the man his father was arguing with, but Ray's face had taken on the sort of greenish pallor that one might find in a wax museum or at a funeral service.

Without warning, the man surged into the living room. He grabbed Ebbie by the hair and dragged her up over the back of the chair. She was too stunned to put up much of a fight. There was a glint of silver, and Charles realized that the man held a gun to his mother's head. From the long barrel and swept-back grip, he guessed it to be a Colt Huntsman. He racked his brain – did this pistol have any quirks or weaknesses he could use in his favor? Foreboding washed over him as his eyes scanned up to the man's face, and he really looked at him for the first time.

It was the man from the bridge party.

The tall man wheeled and snapped at Charles and Ray. "Don't you try anything funny!" Turning back to Fred, he growled, "Where is the money? I *will* shoot her."

Fred snorted. "Go ahead. I've been wanting to do that for years."

The sharp crack of the pistol shattered the air, as well as Ebbie's skull.

In an instant, the man turned from a tall murderer to an armored monster. Two clear, fang-like stems shot of out the thing's mouth, one inserting itself into the entry wound and the other dripping slime onto the floor. It was so tall that it had to stoop against the eight-foot ceiling, and Ebbie dangled like a rag doll in its pincers.

Fred tried to bolt for the front door, but the beast easily snagged him by the arm with one of its clawed legs. Charles heard a crunch, and the old man yelped in pain. Raymond tried to run for the back door, but tripped over debris on the floor and skidded across the linoleum, where he cowered in a corner, arms over his head.

Charles couldn't get up from the couch, and the demonic creature stared him in the eye while it began to suck Ebbie's blood through the mouthpart that it had inserted into the bullet hole in her head. Waves of nausea and terror buffeted Charles as he watched, helpless, as his mother's corpse was desecrated before his stunned eyes.

The monster put a spiked cheliped on each of Ebbie's shoulders, then one at each hip. It had to raise Fred off the ground to keep him from gaining any purchase on the floor. A slime-covered mandible protruded from its head and encircled Ebbie's throat. With what sounded like a single crunching snap, the head and limbs fell to the floor in a bloodless heap. Then it deftly turned the torso and slashed at the abdomen. Sickening wet noises accompanied the awful proboscis as it rooted around in Ebbie's entrails. Charles had to close his eyes as the thing found the liver and gobbled it down, brown globules of the organ sticking to its skull-like face. He gagged at the stench as bowel and stomach contents spilled out into the air.

The greedy creature dropped Ebbie's body to the floor and swung Fred into place for the same treatment.

"Charlie!"

Charles cast his eyes across the room, away from the carnage. Betty stood there, waving her arms to get his attention. Ebbie stood behind her, looking from one hand to the other, confusion on her face.

"Charlie, you have to get the gun!"

"I...I don't think that will work against this thing." A tear slid down his cheek. He supposed Raymond would be next, then himself. Charles had hoped to fall asleep one night soon and never wake up, but not even Fred deserved to die in this thing's terrible grasp.

"It will work. The eyes! Aim for the eyes!" Betty shouted, her wispy voice echoing in his head.

Fred struggled hard against the entity, flinging his head back and forth. A lobster-clawed leg closed around it and squeezed. The shape of his skull changed suddenly and dramatically, bulging out above the pincer.

Charles had to fight back the impulse to vomit as the two fangs protruded and jabbed into his father's eyes, blood spattering on the paper Ray had abandoned on the floor. Fred squealed and shuddered as the venom burned through his body, then he went limp.

Muscles shaking, Charles slid to the floor. He only had a minute or two to find the gun before the beast was done with Fred and ready to move on to its next buffet item.

Metal gleamed under the edge of the end table where the gun had fallen when the tall man had shifted into the monster. He pushed his rigid body the short distance across the floor and reached for the weapon.

But the gun was useless. He couldn't close his fingers around the grip and he certainly couldn't pull the trigger.

Charles whimpered as Fred's limbs rained down on him. His father's head landed on top of his, then rolled away a few feet, ruined eyes staring up at the ceiling.

The monster had trouble removing one of Fred's legs – perhaps it was the arthritic buildup that made it thick and tough. It severed the leg at the knee and placed another claw on the hip joint, scraping away much of the soft tissue from Fred's lower body, and the leg relented. Defeated, it dropped into the grisly pile at the thing's feet.

Slurping.

Ray wept softly in the corner. Charles felt his gorge rise again, tasting bile and acid as he choked back the vomit. He did the best he could to slide the gun across the floor to his cousin, but with his limited range of motion, it barely went halfway.

"Ray!" he bellowed. "Get the gun!"

But Ray curled himself tighter into a ball.

The demonic creature made a hoarse, grating noise. Was it laughing at him?

Charles felt the pressure of its heavy chelipeds on his rocky skin. He rotated as it picked him up so that the fingers of his outstretched arms stabbed at the monster's eyes. It pulled away from him, and tried to bend Charles' body, but his nearly inflexible joints did not yield. Hissing loudly, it set to work severing the offending appendages from Charles' body.

"Ray! Ray! For God's sake! Get up! Get the gun!" The pressure of the pincers on Charles' toughened skin was excruciating.

One of the claws cracked. The monster howled with pain and rage, letting go with the injured cheliped and quickly replacing it with another.

The crack of a pistol shot made it swing around towards Ray. For a moment, it forgot about Charles.

"No!" Ray screamed. "Get away from me!" He fired wildly at the monster, but the bullets ricocheted off its tough skin. Charles felt heat and pressure as a few shots hit him, chipped off a bit of his hard exterior, and bounced harmlessly to the floor.

"Stop!" Charles screamed. Ray had to be down to the last round or two in the magazine. "You have to get its eyes!"

Ray shook so hard that he could barely stand, and Charles doubted very much that his cousin had any hope of hitting his mark.

The creature dropped Charles and moved toward Raymond. He squeezed off the final two rounds, and kept pulling the trigger. Click click click click... The monster was toying with him now, moving closer, circling one way then the other.

Charles slithered through the pile of body parts and wedged himself against the couch to force himself to his feet. He looked around wildly for a weapon, something, anything.

His eyes fell on Fred's leg.

The arthritic one, with all the calcifications and sharp bone spurs. It was large enough that he might be able to grip it.

The monster slapped the gun out of Ray's hands, and Charles watched in horror as it caressed his cousin's shivering face with one massive claw.

The leg lay on top of the stack. Charles struggled to pick it up. Something inside of him snapped, like concrete under a sledgehammer, and he fought for breath. But he could bend enough to pick up the limb now. He knew he had one chance.

"Hey, you! Bug! Turn around!"

The entity stopped tormenting Ray and slowly turned its head toward Charles. Perhaps it would have grinned, if it had flesh on its ghastly face.

Charles hurled the leg as hard as he could. He didn't have the flexibility to draw his arm well back and power it at the beast. The arc of the leg's last-ditch flight bent downward before it reached the monster. Despair swallowed Charles.

But then Ebbie was there. Betty, too. They took hold of the leg and guided it to its mark. For a moment, the monster stood stunned, then it roared and clawed at the femur protruding from its head.

"Ray! Help me!" Charles moved so that Fred's foot was flat against his chest. "Push! Push!"

Ray ran to Charles, put his back against his cousin's, and shoved for all he was worth. The monster's eye socket gave way with a crunch of bone and chitin as Fred's thickened femur penetrated its head. It collapsed to the floor, shuddering and convulsing, its horrible legs flailing in its death throes.

When the monster finally stopped twitching, it started bubbling furiously, creating a slimy froth.

Ray grimaced. "Ugh! Smells like spoilt eggs."

After a few minutes, the reaction slowed and the foam started to dissipate, leaving behind a bubbly mess of offal. Charles felt a new wave of nausea when he realized that must be the partially digested remains of Fred and Ebbie.

The pile of entrails moved. Something was digging its way out of the stinking heap. Ray gasped as a distorted human skull, no bigger than a thumbnail, emerged from underneath a coil of intestine. The rest of it followed, and it shook its body like a wet dog. It wasn't large – perhaps three inches. Aside from the grotesque head, it looked like an ordinary scorpion.

Ray tried to smash it with the butt of the gun. The blows had no effect, and he narrowly avoided being stung.

"It…needs…a host." Betty was scarcely more than a mist, hovering near Charles. He glanced around, but there was no sign of Ebbie.

Charles eyed the scorpion. "A host? It's a parasite?"

"Yes. You…must…trap it. Out…of…energy." The mist started to fade.

"Betty! Wait!"

"Can't…See…you soon…Charlie."

The wispy blur of Betty's last energy evaporated.

"Get a cup or something, Ray!" Charles kept his eye on the parasite that marched steadily toward his foot.

Muttering to himself, Raymond disappeared into the kitchen. Charles hoped he didn't keep going and run out the side door. The scorpion hopped up onto his ankle.

He waggled his foot as much as he could, but it wasn't enough to shake the thing loose.

"Hurry!"

Dishes clattered in the kitchen, but Ray did not reply.

The arachnid began scaling Charles' leg. He swatted at it, his arms stiff and clumsy, and it easily dodged aside. It had no lips, but he felt it smirking at him just the same.

"Ray! C'mon!"

Charles tried swinging around to scrape the intruder off onto the couch. It darted between his legs and started climbing up his back. He could hear the scuffling of its wicked feet as it ran up the small of his back and between his shoulder blades. A strangled cry escaped his throat as he felt a sharp sting at the base of his neck. Liquid fire washed through his body as each beat of his heart pumped the venom-contaminated blood through his veins. Charles couldn't move, but he could hear the scrabbling of many legs in his hair as the parasite burrowed painfully into the base of his skull.

Ray ran back into the room, waving a dented sauce pan.

"Charles?"

Charles stared, unmoving. He wanted to respond, but couldn't force his body into action.

Ray alternated between swearing and crying. He left for a few minutes and came back with a large bucket. Retching, he used a ladle to scrape the pile of organs into the container.

The paralysis lifted as quickly as it had set in, and Charles fell forward onto the couch. His stiff body bounced just a little, and his nose smacked into the wooden frame under the threadbare upholstery.

"Ow."

"Charles?" Ray whirled to look at his cousin. His fearful eyes scanned the room. "Where is it? Where did it go?" He helped Charles to his feet.

"Check the back of my neck. It's in there! Can you get it out?"

Ray ruffled the hair on the back of Charles' neck. "I don't see nothin'."

"I felt it! It got inside my head." His voice broke, and Raymond took a step back.

"What are we going to do?" Ray sounded like a lost child. "Call the po-lice?"

"And what are you going to tell them, Ray? That a giant lobster devil cut my parents up, but we escaped? You're on probation already. And what if the monster –" He couldn't allow himself to finish the sentence.

"I don't know what to do!"

Charles' eyes lingered on the pile of body parts in front of him. "You call cousin Melvin, tell him Ebbie was looking for him. He'll come around to talk to her, and he can call the cops." He sighed. "We can't just leave them out here to rot. Help me put them in the fridge. That has to be better, doesn't it?" The truth was, Charles was starting to feel a surge of strength rush through him, so maybe this parasite had a use, after all.

Fred and Charles had been adversaries for as long as Charles could remember. He didn't feel a sense of loss – how could he lose what he'd never had? – as he stacked the remains of Fred's mortal coil in the icebox. But it was different with Ebbie. True, their relationship was, at best, rocky. Still, he'd once been part of her flesh, and holding her severed arms in his hands shrouded him in melancholy. He stroked her grey hair as he gently placed her head in the vegetable crisper. "I'm so sorry, Ebbie. It shouldn't have been like this."

When Charles closed the refrigerator door, the appliance rocked against the wall, thudding into the brittle sheetrock.

"Cuz?" Ray took a few steps back and glanced toward the door.

"This thing's just rickety. Never was balanced properly." Charles was shocked by the ease with which the lie had slipped out of his lips. He could feel a strength building in him, and was afraid it would end up being more than he could contain. He rubbed his nose.

Ray's eyes widened so much that Charles wondered if they would pop out of his head. "What?"

"You...you scratched your nose."

"What of it?"

"You ain't been able to bend your arm that much in months."

Charles swallowed. He felt sure that the evil thing buried in his skull was responsible for the loosening of his joints. It must be trying to take him over. Was his rocky hide slowing it down and keeping Ray alive? "I don't exactly know how this thing works. Betty said we had to trap it. I think it's trapped inside of me. It's trying to change me. I feel...different." Even his newfound strength didn't ease the pain he felt with every breath, and he knew that Betty was waiting for him – she'd said so, hadn't she? There was no reason for him to suffer any more.

Ray snatched at the nearest weapon, raising a broom as if it were a baseball bat.

Charles laughed bitterly. "I think...I think you're going to have to kill me."

"Oh, no! No, no, no, no, no. Then that nasty bug will dig itself into my head. No."

"Not here. Of course not. I own a couple of lots off Alameda Road, near that new sports stadium they just put up. As soon as it gets dark, that's where we're going. And bring a spade."

Charles spent a little time futilely tidying up the kitchen. Ray had taken to carrying the Huntsman pistol around. Just in case. He had scavenged through the tall man's clothes and found an almost full clip in one of his pockets. Charles doubted Ray's aim would be any better the second time around, but he said nothing. He'd probably do the same, if their situations were reversed.

"I think it's probably dark enough, Ray."

Raymond took a long look out the kitchen window and sighed deeply.

"Wait. Before we go, there's a snapshot in a frame on the nightstand in my room. Abigail, that girl from Canada I told you about."

"I'll get it." Ray trotted up the creaky stairs.

When he returned, he had the picture, but not the gun. Charles supposed it didn't really matter. It would take a much better marksman than Raymond to do the monster any harm if it did manage to take him over. He took one long, last look at the kitchen and closed the door for the final time.

Raymond grunted as he jumped on the back of the shovel. It barely penetrated the concrete-hard gumbo clay.

"Let me try." Charles' voice had deepened.

Raymond handed the spade over reluctantly. Despite his parasite-enhanced strength, Charles couldn't make much more headway than his cousin. At this rate, it would be lunch time tomorrow before they got more than a foot or two deep.

"I have an idea. Let's get in the car."

"Where we goin', cuz?" Suspicion edged Raymond's voice.

"Astrodome. It just opened – but maybe they still have a piece or two of heavy equipment out there."

Ray nodded slowly, doubtful. But if he had a better idea, he didn't come out with it. They drove the short distance to the stadium. As they cruised around the perimeter, Charles couldn't help but marvel at the colossal structure. "What will they think up next? The boys down at NASA are putting men in space, and Houston's got its very own indoor baseball field. It's a crazy old world, huh Ray?" He suddenly found himself reluctant to leave it.

"Sure thing. There ain't no backhoes here. Now what?"

"I just want to get out for a minute and look around."

Ray groaned and pulled the car over to the curb.

Charles got out and looked up at the heavens. The moon was barely a fat crescent, but the Astrodome loomed bright, even in its meager light. He walked across the sidewalk and leaned against one of the trees. It wobbled just a little. The trees had been planted, but only a few had been staked.

"Who are you?" Ray screamed.

Charles whirled.

His cousin brandished something, a piece of concrete perhaps, at a figure in a white cloak.

"It's okay, Ray. I know her." His cousin didn't lower his arm. Not much Charles could do about that. "It's been a long time, Orco."

"Perhaps. You seem to need my help."

"Who is this?" Ray demanded.

"Long story. Someone I met back in my Navy days. She turns up now and then."

Orco pulled her hood down and her dark hair fluttered in the passing breeze. "You are correct. The earthiness of your body holds the parasite at bay. But it will take you over, eventually. You will be nothing more than a husk, a costume it wears to stalk its prey."

"How do you know about that? Are you working with that thing?" Ray's voice cracked with near-hysteria.

"I can see it." She took a step closer to Charles and brushed her fingers along the back of his neck. He groaned and dropped to his knees. She shook her head. "It makes a bad master."

"I don't care about all this mumbo jumbo. We need to get out of here. There's bound to be security guards."

Ray reached for the car door. "Maybe they've already called the po-lice and we just don't know it yet."

"You're free to go," Orco said.

Ray got into the car and started it. He opened the door and half stood, tossing a small metal object at Charles. Orco deftly caught it with one hand. It was Abigail's picture.

That, and the acrid smell of burning rubber, were all that Ray left behind as he peeled out of the parking lot.

Orco handed the photograph to Charles. "This…will be unpleasant. I am sorry for that. But it will not last long."

She waved one hand toward the closest tree. The ground rippled around it, as if it were liquid, and the tree fell over. A hole gaped in its place, then grew wider and longer and deeper. The surrounding earth swayed under the thin moon, a grassy pond. Orco gestured toward the grave, for that's what it clearly was.

Charles could think of nothing he wanted to do less than get in that hole. "There must be another way."

"I am sorry."

Pain flashed through Charles' shoulder. It had tried to move, seemingly of its own volition, too fast and too far. He clutched at it with his other hand. Instead of comfort, he found pain. One of his hands had partially converted to a spiny cheliped.

"No!" Horror drenched Charles' cry.

"Only you can stop this. It is in flux. Stop the transition and it becomes trapped."

"Forever?"

"Probably not."

"How long?"

Orco shrugged. "Hard to say how long it will sleep. A day? A century? But that does not matter if you let its transition continue."

Charles' tears glistened in the moonlight as he forced himself into the pit. He watched the silver crescent for a few moments, until it disappeared above the liquid earth that covered his face. He struggled for air, but sucked in more of the flowing dirt. He tried to cry out, but it poured into his mouth, filling his throat. He clawed at it, but the pressure of its increasing weight pinned his arms. Only a few minutes passed before he stopped struggling.

When the security guards made their rounds ten minutes later, everything looked just the way it had the last time they were there, and they walked on, oblivious to the danger that slumbered in the soil, inches from where they passed.

19

He's not the killer," Mitchell said.

"I agree," Cazares answered as they walked down the hallway to the situation room. Swann hurried to keep up. "What makes you so sure?"

Mitchell slowed his stride, just a little. "The killer is cold-blooded enough to dismember his victims, exsanguinate them, and relocate the remains. This guy wet himself before we could even question him. I don't see someone with that lack of control being able to pull off these murders."

Cazares pushed the conference room door open. A clump of disheveled investigators clustered around a laptop.

"Quetzel!" Ilyn waved them over. "You gotta see this."

They jostled their way into the crowd, and Ilyn rewound the video back to the beginning. "Store across the street from one of the busier prostitute rows. This guy here, Vincente Aguilar, he's the second victim. He starts talking to this girl, the one with the pink hair. They seem to come to an agreement, and walked off together around the corner. Okay, now watch."

Every head, customer and service provider, whipped around in the direction where Aguilar and his lady of the evening had disappeared. They moved slightly in the opposite direction, then business continued as usual.

"What do you suppose they heard?" Ilyn fast-forwarded the recording. The young woman returned from around the corner, but she was alone. She dropped a plastic grocery bag into the bed of a parked pickup truck as she passed.

Could that be the victim's clothes? "And how do we know that he didn't just leave the scene another way?" Quetzel asked, unimpressed.

"We don't. However," Ilyn clicked on another video. "Look at this."

"Same girl," Swann said.

Quetzel stifled a yawn. Three hours of sleep didn't go as far as it used to. *Same girl, same outfit. Same pink hair. Pink hair. What had the homeless witness said? 'She was pink.'*

Ilyn fast-forwarded until a black SUV pulled up. A brief conversation ensued, then the hooker got into the car. "And that vehicle, of course, belongs to our latest victim, Sandy O'Reilly."

"Interesting." Mitchell had shifted his weight so that he was close enough for Quetzel to feel the heat radiating from his body.

A peal of thunder rattled the windows, making Quetzel jump. "Can we isolate and get a still of her? Patrol can canvass the working girls and see if anyone knows her. She's got pink hair – can't be that hard to find."

Ilyn paused the video. "Already on it."

In the moment of silence, Quetzel's stomach gurgled loudly.

"Didn't you have some fancy dinner to go to earlier?" Ilyn teased.

"Funny how a DB can ruin your plans."

Ilyn studied his shoelaces for a moment.

"It's almost twelve," Mitchell said. "I haven't eaten either. What's open this time of night?"

"Whataburger drive through is probably closest."

"Well, if you're going…" Ilyn reached for his wallet.

Cazares and Mitchell ended up taking orders for half the room.'

Torrential rain lashed the windows. Cadence stretched his tall frame as much as possible in Quetzel's cramped cube after he'd thrown the trash from his fast-food meal in the garbage can. "Did you say you had found cold cases with a similar MO?"

"Yeah. There were nine from 1959 to '64, mostly in Texas and New Mexico. Couple in Georgia and Ohio. Only one decedent was identified, because the killer left the head. In Fort Bend County, about thirty miles south west of here, they found a torso of a man lying in a field. There was another one here in town that didn't make that list, from…I believe it was '62. Only skeletal remains of a woman's head." She stifled a yawn. "A multi-jurisdictional task force believed their nine murders were related, but none were ever solved. The big cold case I have is from

1965. Kinda famous – press called it the 'Icebox Murders,' because the dismembered body parts were found in their owners' refrigerator. You wouldn't believe how many books, TV shows, and websites there are about it."

"I can imagine. I'd like to look at the file."

Quetzel shuffled through the stack of folders and binders on her desk. "You know what? I think I left it on my desk at the house. It's way late, anyway. I've got to get home and feed my cat. Can I drop you at your hotel, or do you have a rental?"

"Rental's at the hotel – Swann picked me up."

"What hotel? Near the Green Monster, I guess?"

Mitchell smiled at the reference to the FBI building, then took the card key out of his wallet and gave Quetzel the address. "Is it too far out of your way to stop by your house and grab the files?"

There are faster ways home than via 290 and the Loop, especially in the rain. "It's a little out of the way, but not too bad. You sure you want to look at those tonight?"

"If it's not too much trouble."

"No. It's fine."

Nights like this made Quetzel grateful for her attached garage. Gato met them at the door. He ignored his owner and rubbed his face and body against Mitchell's legs.

Quetzel raised an eyebrow. *Little ingrate.*

Mitchell scooped the kitten up, and Gato purred loudly. Quetzel dropped her bag on the loveseat and went to check the cat's food dish. Half full. Water full.

"Is he your only cat? He needs a buddy."

"That what he's telling you?" *That's just what I need – to be the neighborhood cat lady.*

Quetzel closed the open binder on her desk and stacked a manila folder on top. "I'm just going to use the bathroom, then I'll run you to your hotel."

"Sure. Take your time."

When Cazares returned from her pit stop, Mitchell was lounging in her recliner with Gato sleepily kneading the agent's thigh. He didn't notice – he was asleep. She started to wake him. The lights flickered as lightning sizzled through the rain and thunder cracked. She had no will to drive in that mess if it wasn't absolutely necessary.

She did one last email check on her phone. There was something from Bianca and Justin. They had a shared email address that Quetzel doubted Justin ever used.

Dear Sergeant Cazares: We're so sorry to have inconvenienced your working hours with our thoughtless rehearsal dinner. We understand how terribly unimportant it is to meet your child's fiancé's parents. We do hope our wedding on Sunday doesn't interfere too much with your job. Sincerely, Bianca & Justin

Quetzel sighed. *How much of that email had Jorge written?* She reached out and scratched Gato's ears.

"I wish Bianca wasn't marrying Justin. He's a loser, and the whole thing is forcing me to spend time with my sociopath ex. Goodnight, kit."

She covered Mitchell's legs with an afghan and went to her own bedroom.

Gato opened his eyes. He plopped quietly to the floor and padded to the kitchen. His small jaws gaped in a yawn, and he stretched himself, lowering his upper body almost to the floor. He sniffed the food dish. *Meh.* It was okay, if he was really hungry. But tonight, he had a job to do. Quetzel had asked for his help in eliminating a problem, hadn't she? Fresh meat was an added bonus. Hissing at the rain, he let himself out the doggie door.

Quetzel woke up at 6:04. Two minutes later, her cell phone went off.

"Cazares."

Ilyn's voice was soft and hoarse, as if he hadn't slept all night. "Number six. 9000 block of East Almeda."

"On the way."

Quetzel shook Mitchell's foot. "Wake up, Agent. There's another DB."

Gato yawned and stretched, then walked down Mitchell's leg to bump her hand with his head. "Fair weather friend." She scratched between his ears, and his loud, rumbling purr radiated out of his tiny body. "Why are you damp?"

Mitchell also stretched. Quetzel scooped the fluffy feline off his ankles. "There's mouthwash in the bathroom. I'll get you a cup."

In the kitchen, she deposited Gato near his now-empty food bowl. "Guess I'm lucky you didn't gobble up Agent Mitchell in his sleep."

Quetzel emptied a can of food into his dish. The cat's tail flicked back and forth, then he gingerly licked the flaked tuna.

"What, now you're full? Guess there's a first time for everything."

Cazares applied a squirt of hand sanitizer and retrieved a plastic cup from the cabinet.

"Sorry about that, Sergeant. I was a lot more tired than I wanted to admit. Hope I haven't caused you any awkwardness by falling asleep in your chair for the night."

"I doubt anyone will notice, except possibly Swann, but even if they do, it's really none of their business. With six dismembered bodies and one tiny lead, I doubt anyone has the time or energy to speculate about my house guests."

The sun rose pink and gold ahead of them. Mitchell fidgeted with his ID. "I think it's a bad sign. The killings are getting closer together – two in two days now – he's escalating fast."

"What do you think of the female on the security footage?"

"Not sure how she's connected. It's possible that she isn't, but I think it's much more likely that she's involved in victim procurement."

"But you don't think she's the killer?"

Mitchell picked a black cat hair off his white cuff. "No. At least not on her own."

A young man was stowing equipment in the Medical Examiner's van when they arrived. Quetzel pulled in next to it. She wasn't too surprised that he was already wrapping things up – he could practically walk to the scene from his office.

"Morning, Coop."

"You gotta get this guy, Quetz. He's one bad dude." Cooper studied Quetzel's companion.

"This is Agent Mitchell, courtesy of Behavioral Science. Cadence, this is the best Medical Examiner's investigator that you will ever meet – Cooper Morgenstern."

The investigator blushed. "I wondered when they'd call in the Feds."

Mitchell vigorously shook his hand. "You are just the person I wanted to talk to."

This dump site was an unkempt, brushy and heavily wooded vacant lot. Warehouses lined the opposite side of the street.

Quetzel scowled. "How long has this DB been here? How did anyone even find it in all these weeds?"

Cooper straightened. "It's pretty fresh, less than six hours, I think. A truck driver reported a leg lying in the road."

The agent stayed with Cooper, and Quetzel went ahead to view the body.

It wasn't that the other killings had not been brutal – no gentle hand had touched the previous five victims – but this scene was a testament to a new level of savagery. Uprooted saplings lay strewn about, broken branches dangled from the shrubby undergrowth, and deep furrows tore the grass, as if a metal garden claw had scraped across it. The severed limbs were scattered, as if they had been slung away from the torso by a frenzied attacker. The right leg lay in the roadway, and the left was in at least two pieces, with only the calf being found, about two hundred feet away. Like all the other victims, they were bloodless, but on this one, the limbs had been slashed and torn as well as severed. Grass, embedded deep into the lacerations, clearly showed that this was the location where the decedent had been killed. The torso, empty of viscera, was split nearly in half from throat to abdomen. She wracked her brain to recall any recent reports about any large predators escaping captivity – a tiger could do this. Or a bear. And yet there wasn't a drop of blood to be found. Quetzel made a note to ask Cooper if there was a way to completely exsanguinate a body – even funeral home embalmers didn't get at it all. The other decapitations appeared to have been made in a single movement by a sharp instrument, perhaps an ax or sword. On this one, tattered edges of the neck skin hung like a gruesome ruffle from the torso, as if the head had been torn from the body rather than cut. She shuddered. Years of experience were not always enough to insulate against utter depravity. She was glad Swann hadn't arrived yet.

Patrol officers and crime scene investigators were still looking for the right arm, thigh, and the head.

Violence aside, something about this decedent bothered her, like having a word on the tip of her tongue, or trying to remember a dream, even as the details blurred into the retreating darkness. There was something she was missing. Something obvious, but she couldn't quite see it. Was sleep deprivation finally getting the best of her?

Her text chime sounded. *Arm located. Approx 50 yards S-SE from torso.* Quetzel headed into the bushes, making her way over the knot of officers circling an object on the ground.

Quetzel's breath caught in her throat. *Calm down. Lots of people have that kind of tattoo.* An arm lay between two bushes, a spiky tribal tattoo coiled around the bicep, black ink stark against bloodless flesh. Dread clutched at her stomach with icy fingers.

Now that the grey dawn had given away to morning light, the search was easier.

"Over here!"

An officer had found the head. Or at least most of it. One piece, a slab that included most of a profile, dangled from the shrubbery. Another large chunk lay on the ground nearby.

"Oh, God." Quetzel's hand flew to her mouth.

"Are you okay, Detective?" There was a hint of a smirk from the investigator, as if he thought the sight of the mangled head had made her queasy.

That wasn't it. She'd seen worse. But all her years of crime scene investigation did not prepare her for investigating the death of someone she knew. *If Justin is here, where is Bianca?*

Quetzel whipped out her phone and fumbled through the lockscreen.

Dialing…

Connecting…
Ring…Ring…
"What is it now, Mother?"

Quetzel finally exhaled. "Bianca. I'm coming to see you. I'll be there soon."

She tapped *End Call* before her daughter could ask any questions. She closed her eyes, took a deep breath, then looked at the officer.

"I know him."

Hiss face fell and he groped for words. "Oh…I…uh…"

"His name is Justin Forrester. He's – was – my daughter's fiancé. I just saw him last night at the rehearsal dinner."

"I am so sorry."

Quetzel felt weak in the knees, but forced herself to be steady. "They can't see him like this. I don't want them at the morgue."

"I understand."

She didn't like Justin, had never been enthusiastic for Bianca to marry him. But this? She never wanted anything like this for anybody, not even her worst enemy.

She fought the impulse to vomit. "I'm going to go talk to Cooper."

Cazares headed back to the ME's van. Cooper and Mitchell were deep in a discussion on wound analysis. She didn't care. They could talk later.

"Coop?"

He looked startled. "Quetz! What happened to you?"

She swallowed hard. "The DB. He's my daughter's fiancé."

Cooper hugged her. "I am so sorry."

That's what everybody says. But what else was there to say, really? Quetzel pulled away. "Justin. His name was Justin Forrester. I have to go see Bianca."

Cazares put her hand on Morgenstern's shoulder. "I'll inform my daughter. Could you tell the LT to request a chaplain to accompany the officers that have to tell his parents?"

"Sure."

"Is there anything I can do?" Mitchell asked, a comforting hand on her shoulder.

"Catch this SOB."

She called Jorge on the way.

"Bianca ain't up yet, Babe."

"I know she's awake. I'm on the way over. Do not – you hear me?- do not let her go anywhere."

"What's this about?"

"I don't want to talk about it over the phone."

She ended the call.

Tawni-leigh answered the door. "I hope this is important."

"I'm here to see Bianca."

Tawni-leigh nodded toward the staircase.

"What? Not even a hello?" Jorge called after her as she hurried up the stairs. She ignored him.

Knocking as she opened the door, she found Bianca sprawled across her bed, earbuds on and surfing the web on her tablet. Models adorned with ornate hairstyles smiled from the screen.

"Finally. What *is* it, Mother?"

"Bianca, I have to tell you something."

"What?"

Quetzel took a deep breath and let it out. "It's important. Take the earbuds out."

Bianca rolled her eyes and sat up, removing the earphones. "Fine. What?"

"There's no good way to say this. I'm so sorry to have to tell you, but Justin was found dead this morning."

Bianca blinked a few times. "Dead? What do you mean dead?"

"I'm afraid he was murdered."

"That can't be. You're lying because you don't want me to marry him!"

Quetzel sat on the bed next to Bianca. She put her arm around her child, but the younger woman shrugged it off. "How dare you come here and tell me this! I didn't think you'd be so salty about Justin that you'd come here and try to troll me about him. The wedding is happening. You don't have to be there."

"You know what? I wish I was as petty and manipulative as your father, and that this was all a trick. But I was there. I saw him. Officers are on the way to the hotel to inform his parents." *Did I really just tell my grieving child that her father was petty and manipulative?*

"No!" Bianca sobbed.

Quetzel tried hugging her daughter again. This time, Bianca relented.

"What did you do to her?" Jorge growled from the doorway.

"Justin has been killed."

"¿Que?"

"I really don't want to go into the details. He was found dead this morning."

Jorge sat on the other side of Bianca. He, too, put his arms around their daughter. "It's okay Baby. Papa's here."

His hand burrowed against Quetzel's ribs, and she instinctively recoiled from his touch. Bianca shifted away from her mother and buried her face against Jorge's chest. The detective sighed inwardly. She'd lost her daughter to Jorge's pretty lies and hollow promises years ago. But it still stung.

"What's going on here?" Tawni-leigh stood in the corridor, unwilling to cross the threshold, with her arms crossed and an ugly scowl on her face. She made Quetzel think of a barking dog, ready to bite out of fear. She'd let Jorge deal with his wife.

Jorge stroked Bianca's hair. "It's Justin. He's dead."

Tawni-leigh gasped and went pale under her expensive foundation. "Wha-what happened?"

"Let's talk downstairs," Quetzel said. She felt like a fifth wheel here, anyway, now that Jorge had arrived.

The two women made their way silently to the kitchen. Tawni-leigh pulled a bottle of wine from the large chiller that took up considerable real estate in the kitchen.

Quetzel glanced at her watch. Most people weren't even at work yet. "A little early for that, don't you think?"

Tawni-leigh forced a bad impression of a smile. "I need something to take the edge off."

"I hadn't realized that you and your future son-in-law were so close."

"You weren't supposed to." Tawni-leigh laughed bitterly, then sobbed.

Is there no bottom to the dysfunction of this family? Quetzel made no effort to hide the disgust that must surely be showing on her face.

"Please." Tawni drained the wineglass. "Tell me what happened. Was it a car crash?"

"I'm sorry. He was murdered." It did occur to Quetzel that Justin's murder might have been staged to look like the South Loop Butcher – Jorge was certainly capable of that, if he discovered that his trophy wife had been cuckolding him with his daughter's fiancé. It would certainly explain the differences in the death scenes.

Tawni-leigh sat down hard on one of the breakfast table chairs. "Murdered? Who would want to hurt Justin?"

I can think of somebody. "I understand that it isn't easy for you to hear this. But it currently looks like he's the latest victim of the South Loop Butcher."

"Oh, God." Tawni-leigh put her head down on the table and bawled.

Quetzel's phone chimed. It was Swann. "Cazares." She had to put a finger in her open ear so that she could hear over Tawni-leigh's wailing.

"I'm so sorry to bother you when you're home with your family, but there's something you really need to see. There's security footage from the warehouse across the street. Do you want me to email it to you?"

Cazares shook her head. "No. I'm on the way." She put the phone away and turned to Tawni-leigh. "I can't catch the person who did this if I'm just hanging around here. I need to go to work. I'll be in touch."

Quetzel sat at her desk, watching black and white security video on her computer, flanked by Swann and Mitchell. The timestamp said it was 1:13 AM. On the screen, Justin strolled down the sidewalk, talking with a female. *That little shit.* She walked on the other side of him, and it wasn't clear if she was the mystery girl who'd been caught on film at two other scenes, although she appeared to be about the same size. The young lady from those videos had been identified by a couple of the other streetwalkers by her street name of 'Rose,' because of her pink hair. Justin and his paramour disappeared into a gap in the woods, where his dismembered body was found a few hours later. A couple of minutes passed, then Justin staggered out of the clearing, shirt off and pants around his ankles. He fell hard on his face. Someone behind him grabbed his ankles, and dragged him back into the trees, his fingers gouging tracks in the earth. His mouth was open. Was he screaming? A shudder rolled down her back.

Three minutes passed. A leg came flying out of the dark and landed on the road.

Quetzel rubbed her eyes, not wanting to see any more. "Is that it?"

Mitchell squeezed her shoulder. "No. There's more. Fast forward to minute twelve."

Except for an occasional June bug buzzing near the camera, the scene did not change. Quetzel watched the digits roll as she clicked and held the button. 11:52 on the counter. She released the fast forward. Blotting out the scene, a bat flapped by, in search of the insect feast drawn by the street and warehouse lights. She almost missed the pale figure staggering out of the unclaimed woods. The camera was too far away to see the mystery woman's face clearly, but her shirt was torn in several places, and what might have been a bloody scrape trailed from her wrist almost to her elbow. Something dark, probably blood, smeared her face. She took off at an uneven run, limping heavily on her left, heading back the way she'd come, and disappearing from the camera's field of vision within a few strides.

Quetzel clenched her jaw in frustration. "It's a female, but is that Rose?"

Swann turned off the video. "Already been sent to the FBI's facial recognition software."

"You still think a woman's not the killer, Agent Mitchell?"

"I was wrong about that. And please, call me Cade."

"Who's looking for her?"

Swann coughed. "Everybody they could get their hands on."

"Why are we still here, then?"

Quetzel insisted on driving. As they got on southbound 288, the radio crackled. "Officer down! Officer down! Main and Braeswood!"

She stepped on the gas.

The intersection at Main and Braeswood was shut down, and the perimeter stretched three blocks or more on every side. Quetzel pulled up next to a black and white with the lights flashing.

One of the officers standing beside it nodded to her. "Where yat, Cazares?"

She nodded back. "Arceneaux. What's happened? Radio said there was an officer down."

"Yes, ma'am. Dem two Patrols, Harris and Patel, dey found dat Rose girl hunkered down, you know where dem ole trees are 'round the Astrodome? She crawlt unner a hole in de fence and fixed herself a little nest in dere, cher. When dey come up on her, she took off. T-Harris said she jumped straight over dat chain link like a damn deer. She run up on Kirby Road, and dey was about to catch her up, but she had a rock or quelque chose, and throwed it de officers. It don' matta none – dat T-Harris ova dere, he got de hardest damn head I eva yet seen. He be a'right – don't know 'bout dat rock, doh."

"What about Rose?" Swann asked.

"That coullion be out onna bridge. They dun callt de hostage negotiator to talk her down, last I heard."

"Thanks, Arceneaux."

"Yes, ma'am."

They stopped by the ambulance on the way to the bridge and checked on Officer Harris – he was concussed, but otherwise fine.

Rose, on the other hand, was in a tough spot.

Both ends of the bridge were blocked by police Tahoes, and one side had an armored personnel carrier.

With the recent rain, Brays Bayou was swollen and moving fast underneath the bridge. Rose had two choices, surrender or go over the side, into the flood. She had climbed halfway up onto the guardrail, and was rocking back and forth. Her flesh was too pale, and there was a large dark gash across her face from cheekbone to chin. She chattered to herself, not loud enough for Quetzel to make anything out, though. Rose groaned loudly, and started clawing at her left arm. Blood stained her skin. "No, no, no, no!" Like a trapped animal, she looked over the bridge, then at the blockades on either end.

Swann shook her head. "What do you think she's on?"

"No telling." Quetzel was pretty sure she knew how this would end, and it wouldn't involve a peaceful surrender.

"I'll try and talk to her," Mitchell said. "I did use to be a practicing psychologist."

Quetzel shrugged. "Not up to me. Ask the Incident Commander." She gestured to a bus that had been customized into a mobile command station. He headed that way.

When Mitchell returned, he was buckling on a plate carrier. A tactical helmet dangled by its harness from his wrist. "The hostage negotiator is stuck in traffic – jackknifed eighteen-wheeler on I-45."

He strapped on the helmet, pulled the mic into place, and started onto the bridge. "Rose?"

She backed away a few steps, sliding down the railing. Mitchell stopped.

"Rose. I know you're scared. Please let me help you."

She shook her head, then clawed at her throat. Her skin peeled away and hung in strips from her chest.

"What on earth?" Quetzel looked at Swann. "You think she's got some kind of flesh-eating bacteria infection or something?"

"I have no idea."

Mitchell worked his way slowly toward Rose. She had stopped retreating, but didn't seem any more willing to talk to him.

Without warning, she leapt at him. *That had to be an optical illusion.* She seemed to stretch out to nearly twice her height. He raised his arms to protect his face, then ducked out of the way, rolling to the pavement. Now she stood in the middle of the road, her whole body heaving with every breath. And Cadence Mitchell was no longer in the way. A sniper's bullet slammed into her back, then another, red stains blossoming on her pink shirt. She fell to her knees.

Everything suddenly happened in slow motion. Officers rushed in from either side of the bridge. Rose struggled to her feet, then dragged herself to the railing. The closest officer clutched at her ankles as she heaved herself over, leaving a bloody smear along the metal. But he came up short. Rose splashed into the bayou, struggled as she was carried away by the rushing water, and went under.

"Hey, Tiki! You 'bout ready to pack up?"

"Sure, Leo. I'll drag the cooler and chairs back up to the car, you get the fish divvied up, huh?"

Leo stood and reeled in the line that had been bobbing in the bayou. The high water had also brought a lot of debris with it, and he seemed to have caught more plastic bags than fish today. Still, they had a couple of gar and half a dozen perch — more than enough for tonight's dinner, even split between him and Tiki. "Yeah, I hear the game warden's been getting kinda persnickety lately. Charley told me he got a citation the other day. Best get while the gettin' is good."

Tiki grunted as he hauled the half-full cooler up the steep hill. Leo had kept the stringer of fish in the shade under the bridge, and he picked up a bucket to fill with water to get the catch home.

"Ow! What the—?" Something had stung him. At first, he thought it was a wasp. But then he saw the scorpion. It had a weirdly deformed head, almost like a human skull, and he aimed to crush it with his heel. Only he found he couldn't move. The only thing he could do as the creature scrambled up his clothes was make a *kuh, kuh* sound as he inhaled and saliva pooled under his tongue.

When Tiki came back, he found Leo waiting for him in the shadows. He leaned in to grab the bucket, but noticed it was empty. "You okay, man?"

"Sure, Tiki. I'm fine. Just a little hungry."

Tiki should have run.

If you enjoyed the book, please consider leaving a review at your favorite book site – it helps others find it. Thank you.

Author's Note

Charles, Betty, Edwina "Ebbie", and Fred Rogers were all real people – in fact Fred, Ebbie, and Betty are buried in the Historic Hollywood Cemetary in the Heights. Also real: cousin Raymond Smith, the Maceo brothers, and Jackie Freeman. While Sergeant Cazares does reference actual serial murder cases, all other characters are completely fictional. However, I did extend every effort to make sure that Charles' chapters were as historically accurate as I could make them. On reading an article from the Houston Chronicle dated June 24, 1965, I noted a reference to the Icebox Murders as being the third dismemberment murder in three years. I did find the other two cases in the Harris County Medical Examiner's online Unidentified Decedent notices. The skull of a black female was found on 11/01/1962 (HCME Case Number ML62-2119) and the torso of a white male was found beside the road in Fort Bend County on 06/11/1964 (HCME Case Number PA64-0008/FBCSO Case Number D-2-51664). This led me to an article about nine unsolved dismemberment murders from 1959-1964 on the MysteryMachine.us (formerly officialcoldcaseinvestigations.com). Whether or not these killings are in any way connected to the Icebox Murders, I do not know. But there was a spate of dismemberment killings happening in that time frame, and the killer or killers were never caught.

A similar unsolved case is the Cleveland Torso Murderer (aka, the Mad Butcher of Kingsbury Run), in which at least twelve (but possibly as many as forty) victims, most of whom remain unidentified, were slaughtered and dismembered in Cleveland, OH, from 1935-38.

Keep in touch on Facebook:
https://www.facebook.com/ScaryDetective/

Or visit Black Mare Books: http://blackmarebooks.com

www.ingramcontent.com/pod-product-compliance
Lightning Source LLC
Chambersburg PA
CBHW022127170626
46808CB00002B/885